Light Beyond the River

Light Beyond the River

Encountering the Sacred
from the Center to the Edge

JANIS CONSTABLE

RESOURCE *Publications* · Eugene, Oregon

LIGHT BEYOND THE RIVER
Encountering the Sacred from the Center to the Edge

Resource Publications
An Imprint of Wipf and Stock Publishers
199 W. 8th Ave., Suite 3
Eugene, OR 97401

www.wipfandstock.com

PAPERBACK ISBN: 978-1-6667-4126-1
HARDCOVER ISBN: 978-1-6667-4127-8
EBOOK ISBN: 978-1-6667-4128-5

VERSION NUMBER 081522

To all on the journey
from the center to the edge—and back.
May you encounter the Sacred.
May you be graced by the Holy Lovelight,
every step of the way.

Contents

Light Beyond the River

Encountering the Sacred, from the Center to the Edge

Entangled in the Spiritual Realm—identity unclear
Discernment, crossroads, paths unfold—and heightened are my fears.
It's time to listen and to trust—to open eyes and ears
The still small voice might yet be heard in the music of the spheres.

Below me waits the whimsical pond—still waters do run deep
It holds an ever-living world—a hushed and quiet niche.
Beneath this scene an energy churns where consciousness 'becomes'
Bear witness to transforming change where Light and Life are One.

Above me drifts the indigo sky—a rich auroral dome
Expansive host of wisdom—truth—Contemplatives 'at home'.
Arising in the limitless space—the grand ethereal muse
A feast of knowledge, insight, grace—Prodigious worldly views.

Within me rests the deepest of wells—a wellspring crude and vast
Where echoes of Eternal Sounds—rise up from eons past.
Profound the Celtic sagacious voice—so resonant and real
Whose ripples surge as Sacred Truths—fresh mystical appeal.

Around me stands the great central grove—of forest lore and clime.
So palpable the Presence is—serenity divine.
Surrounded now in liminal space—on thresholds of my faith
Where Holiness pervades my being—delights my tender Faith.

Where meadow meets the fair forest edge—where Light and dark do play.
Safe from the storm and all that harms—where I can find my way.
Where cooing sounds of mothering doves fall peaceful on my ears
Awash I am—my soul ascends—I trust. I'm loved. No fears.

Before me stands the Altar of Rock—Its Holy Lovelight calls
Grand rocky outcrop rising through the woodland hallowed halls.
In front of me such mystery rides—numinous pure and true
Enlightenment, encouragement, and wonderment ensue.

I turn for home—the river so deep—three muses in my head
Enlivened by my journey now—grounded, grateful in debt.
Sojourning free in comfort and peace—to rest, to breathe, renew
My Sabbath in the Center? Edge?—to contemplate, to muse.

Beyond the river beckons the Light with mystical allure
It draws my curiosity—I come, intrigued for sure.
May I be opened to its sweet call—in body, mind and soul
May I be changed, transformed—transcending—becoming truly whole.

Throughout my being, my essence, my soul, suffusing all I am,
Reside the mysteries of life, the truth of who I am.
In golden spirals, golden threads and golden mystic webs,
I rest, I wait, I come to see, the here and now, the next.

I'll journey from my center, my home—out to the farthest edge
That's where I'll witness every realm—and vow to build my nest
The River, Lovelight, Celtic Thin Place—three muses I hold dear
I'm called to listen, poised to hear—the music of the spheres.

Janis Constable 2020

Pronunciation Key

Lyra	LEER-ah
Saye	SAY-yee
Saoi	SAY-yee
Paidi	PIE-dee (sounds like Heidi)
Zoli	ZOH-lee
Yala	YAH-lah
Bradn	BRAH-dun
Crea	CRAY-yah
Jovi	JOH-vee
Xavad	Shuh-VAD
Aorla	OR-lah (the first A is silent)
Chalcedony	Kal-SEH-dun-eee
Cruith	CROO-ith
Zaba	ZAH-bah (sounds like Abba)
Diarama	Dee-YAR-ah-mah

PROLOGUE

Details Matter

Meet Lyra—The Poet Who Lives by the River

Entangled in the Spiritual Realm—identity unclear—
Discernment, crossroads, paths unfold—and heightened are my fears.
It's time to listen and to trust—to open eyes and ears—
The still small voice might yet be heard in the music of the spheres.

Ahhhhhh—Home sweet home. Home is where the heart is. Home is the endearing word for where the heart dearly longs to be. Many famous people—presidents and prime ministers, poets and sages of our time—have all tried, in their impassioned speeches, to find just the right expressions to articulate the sentiments of home. The yearning for home, the aching to be home, and the safety and security of being home are all small parts of it. Home is a simple, yet complex place, or space, or time. Home is the manor of the heart—the place where body, mind and spirit find the comfort of connectedness, of belonging, of nurturing rest. Home is the very center—the hearth and haven—of well-being. Home, is that restorative realm, where we feel most centered, balanced, and whole. Home hearkens. Home heals. Home calls us home.

So, how is it that we wander? How does our wanderlust manage to lure us away when the magnets of home are so powerful and strong? How is it that our adventures begin when we close the door of familiar comforts behind us, and we take our first steps away from the hallowed halls of home, into the grand mysteries of life's unknown? Because we are all on a personal quest of knowing, of learning, of being—and of becoming. Perhaps then in being something, and in becoming something, we are intentionally forming ourselves, on our journey toward becoming most fully human. Hmmmmmm . . . .

◎◎◎◎◎

The riverside was a rhythmical and harmonious place to call home. Running waves would crest upon the shores, as the waters would eternally lap and ebb and flow. Time streamed like water—fluid, dynamic and sure.

Lyra, was a nurse by profession and poet by passion and gift. She lived by the River Saye, at the mouth of the river into the Bay of Saye, in the Buchanan Lakes District of Central Canada. This idyllic abode was the home of her own desire, and of her own choosing. Her family home for generations had been very nearby, in the heart of the village of Buchanan Lakes.

Lyra was a remarkably compassionate, free spirited woman, contemplative by nature, mystical in approach, who was truly poetically blessed. Her faith roots ran deep. Her Celtic roots ran deeper. She felt called, beckoned. She felt nurtured, and connected through the Celtic Christian Wisdom. She had a sense of being held and gathered in by her faith. In living by the water's edge, Lyra was naturally drawn into the rhythms of life—into the mysteries of life—into the depth and complexities of all life. The river was indeed her muse.

All of life was relational in Lyra's eyes. All life had purpose, meaning and relationship. It was this relational perspective that allowed her to muse deeply, to see the connectedness and the interconnectedness in all life forms. It gave her an analytical understanding of all life-relationships. It was this relational perspective that allowed Lyra to identify, clarify, mystify, and even personify her own poetic characters and images. Lyra, in her home by the river, for the most part of her adult life, had been contented, confident, and complacent.

Lyra was in her sixties. A young sixty she'd say! Sixty is the new forty! She was healthy and energetic and her mind was very sharp. She was capable of accomplishing whatever she set her heart or mind to do.

Of late, however, Lyra had been noticing a growing restlessness. Disturbing and deeply visceral winds of change had stormed like gale force winds from within her channels and depths. It was a sense of longing and an unexplainable urge to fill her heart and mind and soul with newness, and wonder. She shuddered—she cringed—just at the thought of her second Saturn Return. Her first at age thirty, had been dark and frightening, and tough enough. She needed to, she wanted to, shine brightly. She wanted to shine biblically, like the stars in the grand night sky! She didn't want the glow of her inner Light to be hidden, under a bushel. She wanted her life, present and future, to glow. She wanted it to represent her true inner self. She wanted her inner Light to shine—shine brightly—whatever that meant!

She couldn't put her finger on exactly what was driving this restlessness, so she had allowed these feelings to stew and churn, over time. Her curious heart just needed answers. She felt a comforting calm when she finally articulated these words.

In my retirement, I need a sense of direction and purpose. I feel like I've aimlessly ambled into the infamous intersection in St. John's, Newfoundland—Rawlin's Cross—at rush hour, and I cannot safely take another step. I need to stop. Gather myself, and catch my breath. I need to find my way. I need to name my path and intentionally move forward on my chosen road. And then, I need to rise up and do something good with it—something deeply meaningful in life.

I've already dabbled in the Creative Life, I've danced in the Compassionate Life, and I do double down deeply in the Contemplative Life. Do I need to choose one pathway over the other? Are they conflicting, or holding me back from a wonderful future solely focused on one of these pathways? What are my strengths? What are my gifts? I've been writing for years—Is any of my work worthy of being published? What am I being called to do? How do I choose? What's holding me back from deciding?

I know I need to stop questioning and musing and just make a decision by naming some concrete foundational truths. Maybe I need to take a risk or two. Maybe I need to start to seek a new grounding upon which to build my exciting and shining new world. Possibly a late-life career change? A higher ground? A Holy Ground? A new life perspective? A new framework or paradigm? A new lens through which to perceive all of the wonders of Creation—a new approach—perhaps even a new muse? Hmmmmm . . . .

The region of Buchanan Lakes was a land of hearty living. Originally cleared and settled by the early Scottish settlers to Canada, in the mid to late 1800s, these lands were highly valued, because of their proximity to water. Their easy access to waterways—water route transportation—was an asset. The Dominion Lands Act of 1872 had enticed many settlers to the region—they were all in search of a fresh new start in life, on the Treaty Lands, in the very heart of Central Canada. Mining, forestry and agriculture would eventually become key sources of income for the hardy settler families. Lyra knew of—and was sensitive to—the darker truths of the land acquisition from the Indigenous Peoples. She was acutely aware that modern day words and actions in the name of Truth and Reconciliation, were long-overdue, and ultimately essential in the healing of the nation.

Many rustic family homesteads could be found nestled on the shorelines of the region. The awe-inspiring backdrop of woodlands behind the rocky shorelines, warmed the hearts of any first-time visitor.

There were some breath-taking expanses of Canadian Shield granite rock formations and "craigs"—craggy rocky outcrops. And, there were both lightly and densely forested areas that offered a reverent hush to the passer-through.

The tall straight trees were mostly found in coniferous stands. There were also many mixed deciduous stands, of trees that appeared gnarly and curly. They were twistedly mystical in appearance.

These welcoming, widely spaced broadleaf trees were found in groves at the needled tree forest edges and at the river shorelines. These thin forests were luminous and decidedly alluring. But just behind them, in the central forest depths, the thick central forest was dark and mysterious and somewhat brooding. The true density of the interior forest was actually quite foreboding. The thick underbrush made it difficult for easy travel or touring. Only the very nimble and sure-footed animals could call this central forest, home.

The bedrock layers of the Lake District were laced with a multitude of aquifers. With the water table being usually quite high in all four seasons, pristine spring-fed ponds and ancient natural pure-water wells abounded over the rugged terrain. The glorious River Saye was a wide river confluence of six minor river tributaries flowing southward from their northern highland forest and rocky watersheds, much like the dramatic Highland/ Lowland topography of the original settlers' native homelands in Scotland. It was as if the River Saye received input from the heights and from the depths—and from far and wide—literally from all corners of Creation. Loosely translated from the Gaelic word saoi, meaning sage, the River Saye was mystically all-knowing, carrying with it the waters of wisdom of all time.

It churned its way onward, as a composite mystical beauty in a unique realm of nature all of its own. The watercourse of the Saye held many segments of dancing whitewater rapids and sections of fast flowing currents. Closer to the mouth of the river at the Bay of Saye, however, the elevation of the land notably leveled out, and the river was then seen as wide open. The waters unassumingly, yet majestically, courted the shores in their own oblivious and unhastened time. Time didn't matter. Eternity freshly flowed. The lovely River Saye lyrically danced through all hearts—through all time and seasons—through all realms and runes and greater reason.

It was very true that Canadians witnessed the four seasons in a most vivid way. And Lyra loved just this. The springtime would come as a lush greening, a loamy moisture-laden breath, and a friendly warming embrace by the sun's shortening rays. The summer would dress up in patchwork pockets of golden waving wheat fields, with the perfumes of richly pine-scented forests, bedazzled by the sparkling fresh Temagami-blue waters all around. And the autumn was a magnificent gala, regally resplendent in textures and colors and richness of landscapes. The shimmering shawl of winter was so pure, so iridescently dazzling, just like the whitely luminescent clothes of Jesus at the time of His Divine Transfiguration. Winter was welcomed as a time of renewal, of quiet germination. There was a real and palpable sense of preparation for all of the vibrant seasons yet to come.

Lyra's home was comfortable. She was raised in the comforts of middle-class village life in her early years with her family. In the late 70s, she went away to university, and then moved out to St. John's, Newfoundland for two years before returning to the mainland for her nursing schooling. In her late twenties, Lyra returned to the Buchanan Lakes District, this time to live alone by the river. She was drawn to the rhythm of life on the river. She felt as though she was part of something very much bigger than herself when she moved to the riverside.

The house she chose was most austere and cabin-like. It was snug and warm in the harsh winters, and it boasted a large central stone hearth fireplace by which to curl up. In the sluggish humidity of summer, the cabin was a cool oasis. It was a one-floor home just for her. As there was no guest room, the occasional guest would sleep on her large futon couch, under the sun-faded colors of a homemade cotton quilt. Her home by the river was her sanctuary, her own private haven.

She had deep-seated chairs, both wicker rocking chairs and wooden Muskoka chairs, on her wrap-around screened-in verandas, with views to the river and to the edges of the mystical forest. A tiny babbling brook leant its dulcet musical voice to the northern shady side. The west-facing front veranda offered incredible sunset views over the mouth of the River Saye into the Bay of Saye, in the Buchanan Lakes District. Some folks had hammocks. Lyra had an oversized, hanging basket chair in her woodland garden, where she could spend countless hours gazing over the river, contemplating, and composing. Her chair literally suspended her, swaying in the breeze. She was free in the air, free to just be. Many heartfelt compositions—poems, prayers, stories and songs—were born right there, in her special chair.

The other two sides of her home looked out into the curious deciduous forest. The twisted trunks and branches reminded Lyra of some Irish folk-tales of the leprechauns in the forest, hiding in the gnarly woods. In fun, she would peek around the trees. She'd look and look and look, but alas, she never did lay eyes on any of the mischievous wee Irish lads! They kept themselves out of sight, always busy, using their crafty cobbler skills behind the trees in the forest, while remodeling and mending old shoes. So said the old Irish myths! Lyra could step easily into and out of the real world—in her poetry, in her imagination, in her mystical ways—almost to the point of suspending her self in an alternative reality. It was play. It was her way. It was her world.

Lyra had worked part-time as a Registered Nurse at the cottage hospital, in the village. She loved her work in the ER. Saving lives and helping folks to feel better, was only a small part of her work. Her outstretched hands played catch as they deftly received wee babes when they made their dramatic wailing entrance into the world outside the womb. In the ER, her hands comforted the frail and the dying in their final hours. Her broad shoulders were available to comfort the suddenly bereaved. She listened intently to the broken, to the forgotten, and to the lost. She made timely referrals to counselors for both the new and the returning mental health patients.

Lyra estimated that her daily patient-centered health teaching was one of her most important roles in ER nursing. Cardiac education. New-diabetic or stroke teaching. Hydration and diet review. Wound care. Cast care. Social gynecology issues. Male health concerns. And so much more. Lyra in her late career, had become a walking textbook of all things ER. Her work in the ER was demanding yet at the same time it was fulfilling and rewarding. No two shifts were ever alike, and Lyra surely thrived in the frenetic pace in the world of ER. Adrenaline junkie? Yes!

That being said, there were two very real and very different sides to Lyra. A go-go-go side in her professional world and a laid back, contemplative side, in her personal life. Her two lifestyles were complete opposites, yet there was a healthy balance, in Lyra's eyes. And balance was essential.

The Buchanan Lakes District Hospital was a small outpost nursing station of the Canadian North, with technological links to medical staff and imaging services in nearby centers. Their onsite laboratory diagnostics were limited. Her broad emergency nursing knowledge base made her a valuable asset to the staff. All of her medically complex, critical, and unstable patients were transferred away, for referral to specialists in the larger urban centers. The helicopter transfer service was well utilized in her hometown.

One emergency physician, Paul, was her favorite doctor at the tiny hospital. He was a seasoned professional man, and he was comfortable in his very big shoes. He and Lyra trusted each other implicitly in their professional roles. They were an excellent working team, and they could count on each others' strengths as the emergent needs arose. When Lyra was working, Paul would hail out to Lyra "Good Morning, Saint Lyra!" and she would hail back "Top o' the morning to you, Saint Paul!! Saint Paul the Almighty!"

Not all doctors had been so easy for Lyra to work with. And that's what made Paul's manner and work ethic so special and saint-like in her eyes. One less-than-favorable previous ER doctor in particular had always taken exception to Lyra's patient-focused, compassionate approach to all of her patients and their families. She spent lots of time with her patients. She advocated strongly for the needs of the underdogs and those who had slipped through the cracks—the elders and the marginalized patients. This constantly irritated him and it slowed him down in his work in the ER.

One day he said—to her face, "You're not like all the other nurses, are you Lyra? You are not cut of the same cloth at all. You're old school—a bit of a geek, aren't you? You are a bona fide geek!" His words—although playful and sarcastic—were dead serious, targeted, and hurtful. She much preferred working with doctors of great integrity, diplomacy, and genuine human kindness. Team players.

Lyra had chosen in her early fifties to reduce her workload at the hospital by working only part time. This then freed her up considerably to pursue her passions in her writing, and, to begin to serve her church community as their salaried Parish Nurse. In her ministry, whole-person health in body, mind, and spirit became the focus of her work.

But, by the end of the next ten-year period, commitments and pressures had mounted again, and Lyra noticed the early warning signs of caregiver burnout. She was burning out, and fast. Reactive and curt responses to stressful patients and their families replaced her normal gracious ways. Negativity rolled in, squashing her ever-optimistic persona.

She was tired all the time. Shift-work and long hours were taking their toll. She still loved her work in Emergency and in Parish Nursing Ministry, but her fatigue, her exhaustion, was weighing her down. She lost her desire to write. It took way too much energy and concentration. Her writing just wasn't fun anymore. She'd rather nap and recharge and catch up on some Z's.

So she made another timely decision, this time to retire from nursing altogether. She knew she needed time to recharge, to feel like her old self again. Newly retired, she got a dog. Paidi was a dark-eyed, bright-eyed, wire-haired mutt BFF. Lyra got her as a pup, and at two years old, Paidi was all of 6 pounds. Tiny wee Paidi!

And so her jubilee season began. Upon full retirement at age sixty, she rested long and well. She began to write again, with eagerness and joy. This long-awaited return to her creative realm made her feel whole again, and she welcomed this. She took a few well-deserved retreat weeks, for both learning and personal renewal. During this restorative time, Lyra discovered that she was truly struggling underneath it all, with her identity—with her own perceived loss of identity.

Bingo! Nailed it! Major aha moment!!! That's it! That's the word! My identity! I've been trying to come to terms with the true source of my restlessness. I have just described all the symptoms of a personal identity crisis! I'm not employed anymore. I'm not a nurse anymore. I don't know who I am anymore! Or, who I'll become!

I—me—Lyra—I'm having an identity crisis! In these very words, she settled. She cooled her jets. Loads lifted. *I have a real and tangible reason for my angst. I can name it. I can wrap it up and put it away in a box.* Or, so she thought!

She then asked herself these very direct questions: *What am I? Who am I? What will I become? How do I get started? How do I choose? Is there any truth in the words: "Once a Nurse, always a Nurse?" I don't know what it is, or what it looks like, or where I need to look to find it, but there is for sure, a life after nursing. And I'll be sure to find it!*

It was up to Lyra to act upon this revelation. She contemplated three pathways—The Compassionate Life (some kind of nursing work?) versus The Creative Life (collating and publishing all of her poetry, music and liturgical compositions?) versus The Contemplative Life (applying her mystical mind to the bigger questions, and then publishing her profound and relevant pearls of wisdom?). *Ohhhh, how do I even begin to choose?*

In the well-lit corners of her brain, the scene was set for Lyra's new story to play out. She was about to learn some profound life lessons to guide her through her tensions and through her storms, to lead her into a world of Light as she'd never ever known before. She was about to set out from her home, embarking on a journey from the center to the edge and back! Her time in the now, was hers for the making—hers for the taking—it was, simply, hers.

The story of *Light Beyond the River* begins here. Please slow right down. Enter into every word and into every breath, with Lyra. Breathe deep with Lyra. Open yourself fully to the experience of a God-given odyssey that will warm your heart and light your path—in the depths and in the mystery of an unfolding modern Celtic folklore tale. Leave your rush and your hurry behind. Slowly, slowly, wade in, immersing yourself in Holy wonderment, in wisdom, in story.

From the Depths of the Pond
Meet Zoli—the Celtic Dragonfly

Below me waits the whimsical pond—still waters do run deep—
It holds an ever-living world—a hushed and quiet niche.
Beneath this scene an energy churns where consciousness 'becomes'—
Bear witness to transforming change where Light and Life are One.

Beginning With Prayer

Lyra enjoyed her teatime, daily. Any time of day was teatime. With a notebook and pencil always handy, and her online thesaurus and dictionary only a few clicks away, Lyra would pass away the hours reflecting and writing, for as long as her teapot was full. Her favorite teapot was a very special "Berlin engineered" double-lined aluminum vessel with amazing thermal capabilities. Her freshly poured tea was always hot, hot, hot—even the very last cup! Her all-time preferred tea was loose-leaf cardamom tea. It had the power to calm, comfort, and center her.

Lyra was pensive, sitting curled up on her rocker. Her free and easy long curly locks tumbled and cascaded over her tee shirt, their whites blending in the sparkle of the morning light. Her tiny dog Paidi, was snuggled up in her lap. Lyra toyed with the Celtic braided bracelet, a rose gold bangle around her left wrist—a thoughtful gift from her maternal grandmother. The braid was a powerful symbol in the Bible, in Celtic traditions, and in Lyra's heart. It was a timeless symbol of solid strength, of unity and harmony, and of love.

A small Connemara marble Celtic Cross stood on the table beside her. She was facing outward from the north side of her veranda, beside the brook. The brook was musical, even lyrical at times. Water was everywhere in Lyra's life—in the river, the bay, the brook, the ponds, the wells—and indeed, in the weather! She felt so connected to the water. She often called the river her muse.

The brook was softly chanting in a mesmerizing water babble. Its sonorous waters gave her goose flesh. She was deeply sensitized, yet calm and present, in the moment. She was truly connected to the natural world. But on this day, she also had an annoying and persistent interruption.

She sighed. *Irish Poet W.B. Yeats' ancient poem keeps on circling around in my head like a broken record. His pure poetic imagery "because a fire was in my head" is repeating itself over and over and over again. Well, in Yeats' poem "The Song of Wandering Aengus," the young man Aengus must have had a lot on his mind, for he had a fire in his head, so he went for a walk outside in the nearby mystical woods, to clear his mind and put out his head-fire. So, that sounds like a really great idea. I too need some fresh air. I need to put out the fires in my head. It's time to refresh myself, body, mind and spirit, and a long walk outdoors feels so right. That's just the ticket.*

Remaining seated, Lyra closed her eyes, to enter into a morning prayer of gratitude, before setting out on her impromptu trek into the woods. She stroked Paidi's wiry, wispy fur with gentle loving strokes as she prayed. She spoke to God, in earnest and in gratitude, of her abundant-life blessings. She had read once upon a time, about a unique spiritual practice of visualizing herself sitting in God's lap while praying—while being in conversation with God—while confiding in God in prayer. She had grown to appreciate that visual imagery so very deeply. Endearing images of her childhood days, of her, curled up into her own daddy's lap, warmed her from the inside. She could even recall her own childlike voice and simple words "Guess what Daddy?" or "Please Daddy!" or even "Thank you Daddy." and "I'm sorry Daddy."

In the brightness of a summer morning, comfortably curled up in her rocker, it was just so easy for Lyra to transfer herself—transport herself—in prayer, to the Holy Place, the Comfort Place—in God's lap. She looked at little Paidi, nestled in her lap. The image was so powerful. So very real.

After a few moments in tumbling words of easy-speak, Lyra continued "God, you are with me. You are always with me. Please grace my path today with the warmth and the glow of your precious Holy Lovelight, that I might be safe, that I might grow on my journey. Please help me to sense your Presence within me and around me as I go."

She let her voice trail off. She intentionally lingered in a focused, yet spacious silence for a few for minutes, sensing God's loving Presence. She waited ever-hopefully for a nudge, or a message, or a word of wisdom to ponder. With her eyes still closed, her lips in time, released a warm and gracious "Thank you."

In the sweet mystery of this pivotal prayerful moment, Lyra was deep in her contemplative headspace. On the air of prayer she arose from her chair, setting out on her woodland walk. Lyra set out in to the Light, into the Light Beyond the River.

Holy Moment

It was a bright August Saturday morning. The sky was ultra-blue with puffy cotton clouds drifting in ever-changing shapes and sizes. The weather that morning was glorious. Warm days and warm evenings and no hint of rain for this seven-day forecast. How nice!

Lyra picked up wee Paidi and held all six pounds of her up to her eye level. "Now you be a good girl while I'm gone. There's food and water in your bowls. Remember to use your little doggie door to go outside to the pen if you have any personal business to accomplish. I'll be gone for a while, a good long while. You've always managed well without me when I've gone into town. I'll miss you for sure. I miss you already!" Lyra kissed Paidi's tiny nose and received a sweet little lick in return. "I'll tell you all about my walk—the pond, the falls and the meadow—when I get back! We'll throw sticks in the river when I get home. Ok?" With that, she drew Paidi in to her chest and held her close. Paidi molded herself into the hug. She loved her mommy-hugs.

Lyra set Paidi gently on the floor, and Paidi wandered away, toward the kitchen. Lyra slipped her feet into her well-worn hiking shoes and laced them up. She pulled on a lightweight white sweater, just in case she met some late-season mosquitoes along the way! It was August after all, and the mosquitoes would likely be long gone. In Lyra's mind though, there was no harm in being careful, or prepared. She was always prepared. She tugged at the everpresent elastic scrunchie around her right wrist. Her tresses could easily go into a messy updo if she got too warm.

She unlatched her front door and stepped out of the screened-in veranda, out onto the small wooden porch. The door closed with a bang, behind her. "Bye Paidi! Love You!" She stopped and took in one deep, warm-air breath and let it out slowly, noting the air buzzing through her nostrils. She noticed the tension in her tummy muscles release into total relaxation. She could feel her heartbeat pulsing, tingling, in her fingertips after that one long deep breath.

This is good, really good. I'm energized and my lifeblood is coursing through my veins, bringing oxygen-rich air deep down into the cells of my body. I'm energized. I'm off! She danced down the two wooden stairs, as light as a feather would float, falling whimsically on the breeze. Exhilaration. Anticipation. *Joie de vivre.* She was ready to take it all in, whatever the day would bring.

Hmmmmm . . . . In which direction should I go? It rained pretty hard here, over the past few days. I wonder if the forest floor will be dry? I could stick to the path along the river shoreline, but then I'd chance bumping into neighbors and strangers, and all I want is a quiet nature walk to clear my mind. So, I'll head into the broadleaf woods where the stands of trees are thinner. I'm sure the path will be dry enough in there, in this lovely warm air and gentle breeze. So she walked around to the back of her home and set off on a well-traveled pathway into the forest, away from the river.

It's so pretty in here. I never get tired of the beauty of the earth. And the gnarly trees actually look quite elegant today. Their twisted arms and branches all look like they're reaching out, swaying and waving and welcoming me. Maybe they feel like dancing too!

Lyra grinned. She personified everything in her mind. She found rhythm and rhyme and melody in all spoken words. Music was inherent in the birds and in the trees and in the wind.

Words are magical. My words can paint the images and details that canvas artists simply cannot. Words are never to be used loosely, for each word has its own style and uniqueness, its own character, its own identity and place in the world. All words have their perfect fit, their niche in the world. Personified, words themselves would be tickled pink, and they would royally delight in their being perfectly spoken, written, sung, shouted and cooed! Words, used correctly, can comfort and befriend. They can enlighten and entertain. They can demystify or even mystify! Words have a power, a connecting and engaging power, all of their own.

The path was indeed dry enough for pleasant walking. Lyra's lightweight hiking shoes would most certainly serve her well as she strode out on her spirited jaunt. She thought about her previous nature walks where she would stop a lot along the way to linger in the moments, to savor all of the sounds and the scents, and the sweetness of the space. *I can liken myself on my leisurely walks, to a Flaneuse de la Forêt, or more simply, as a knowing woman idling in the now. I've never been and never will be, a city slicker—for—sure! Maybe a village slicker, or a whimsical "woman about the woods." The word nemophilist, describes me to a T! No haute couture, or salon de coiffure for me!* Words, persona, and identity were important to Lyra. Real words. Real people. Real down-to-earth living.

She was still in the well-lit edges of the forest, when her mind drifted for an instant to a beautiful prayersong that she had written, one that she had affectionately called her personal prayerful mantra. These heartfelt words would often just pop onto her tongue and spill out, when she was overwhelmed with gratitude in her heart—when she could sense that God was with her. She softly chanted the words and released them to the wind as she entered into the mystery of the forest:

> *"In my God I'll be ever thankful*
> *For the Lovelight graces me*
> *Stirring deep within my heart and soul*
> *Leading me through all the darkness*
> *Calling me to walk in Holiness."*

(Sung in quiet prayerful Hesychastic chanted repetition,
striving toward an imminent experiential presence of God)

Lyra always felt a certain connectedness, when she sang these words. She likened her current lightness of heart to the lightness of the veil of tranquility that she had sensed once upon a time, during the singing of a summer-camp Sunday evening vespers prayersong, in the outdoor chapel by the lake at sunset. And today was no different. Her heart was light. Gossamer-light.

She stopped on the path for a moment and closed her eyes. Indeed this was a special moment, in a special time. And she knew she was tuning in with her spiritual senses. She never really knew *how* this happened, or how she could make it happen on command, but she could always identify *when* it was happening to her.

I feel a calmness, an enveloping peacefulness. An inner radiance warms me. An unexplainable feeling like the glow of love, lights my soul. A comforting deep peace is washing over me. I have a feeling of ancient connectedness—in the moment, to the world, to my God, to myself, and to all time and place—connected by something. Like a river is running through my soul and floating me through the ages of all time. Is this buoyed-up moment in time indeed a Holy Moment? Have I just stepped into a Holy Place?

For Lyra—To be in a "Holy Moment" while being in a "Holy Place" and to be so ready and so eagerly open to both of these through her own heightened spiritual senses—well, this was not to be taken lightly. To just shrug it off and say "Huh, well, that was a Holy Moment" and walk away, is not something Lyra would do. She was a Christian by upbringing but warmly and intensely spiritual by her own life experience and passions.

She dearly wanted to dwell in the moment, to linger long in the moment. She wanted to enter into it, fully, wholly, and completely. She looked for just the right rock upon which she could while away some time. There were large lichen-encrusted boulders randomly strewn everywhere in the forest domain. They were leftover evidence of earth's grand upheavals during the glacial ages. She noted that the pond just off to the right of the trail was actually much closer to the trail than ever before.

"Wow!" she exclaimed out loud, "The heavy rains last week and the very high groundwater table have made this pond grow outward in a really big way. Way beyond its normal borders. It's a whole lot bigger than I can ever recall!" Ethereal remnants of the morning mist mystically wisped and wafted over the pond's glassy surface.

Her mind wandered, deeper, wider, farther. *Perhaps the greatly enlarged pond is actually a symbolic expression of my mystical state of being? Or, of my current expansive mindset and my readiness to be connected to my pond milieu? Maybe, simply, God's Presence being with me, makes everything seem bigger, broader, and more blissful? Maybe this super-sized pond is part of or an extension of my Holy Moment?* She breathed in deeply. *God is with me.*

She found a large, level boulder at the water's new edge. The knee-high rock curiously, had a raised upright section at the back to serve as a perfect backrest. *This is one unique rock for me to sit upon for just a few idle moments to take in the wonder of this larger pond. I can just loll away here and attune to this wonderful watery world. Hmmmmm . . . .*

Lyra sat down and realized that she was a bit warm. It was a beautiful day in her forest neighborhood, and she delighted in taking some extra time there on the rock. She unbuttoned, and slipped off her cardigan and folded it neatly. She unlaced each shoe and set them with her sweater on the rocky shelf. Then she dipped her feet in the cool still waters.

"Ooooooohh—that's lovely!" she gasped. "Hello beautiful water," she said to the large pond, "it's lovely to see you today." It was time to empty her head of everything, and time to hold onto the sweetness, the preciousness, and the wonder of her fleeting Holy Moment. She was now ready "to go deep" in her contemplative world.

What's in a Name?

Lyra gazed intently at the still waters. She could see the mirror image of the sun and the indigo sky. She sat in silence, in awe. The moment called her into stillness. She mused for a moment, on what it might be like—what it could be like—to be seated on that very rock, on a brilliant starry night. She wondered, *Might I at nightfall, be able to see the reflection of all the stars, in the depths of this pond?* She smiled at the thought and at her own whimsied ways.

Her mind wandered to the constellations, particularly to the harp-shaped constellation, Lyra, for which she was named. Mythology tells of the great poet and musician, Orpheus, who played the lyre with both perfection and passion. He was known to charm the animals and the birds and the evil ones, with his songs. Upon Orpheus's death, the god Zeus placed Orpheus's lyre in the sky, as a reminder to all through the ages, of the wonders of the great poet's music.

Lyra's paternal grandfather, her Grandpops David Buchanan, was a poet. Her parents chose to honor him by naming their daughter after a great poet. They chose, rather they preferred, the pronunciation as LEER-ah, as it was softer and more lyrical than the alternative, LAI-rah or LAI-ar.

Her middle names Rennie and Rose, were named after her two loving grandmothers, effectively making her initials spell LRR, almost Lyre-like! Her own name was a simple phonetic rendering of a constellation, of the stars. Through her name, Lyra felt connected to her family and to her world, in a poetic sense, in a celestial sense, and most especially in a timeless and eternal sense. To her, her name was an honor, a blessing. Her name was a very special gift, even prophetic.

Attuning

While sitting and savoring her pond scene, a song popped into her head and quickly she chased it out again, because she was so desperately wanting to tune in to the Sacred. "Arrgghh!" she grumbled. There it was again, this time not just the melody, but a few insistent lyrics traipsed around inside her head as well.

And before she could chase it away again, the full-blown lyrics revealed themselves to her, front and center, in her mind. She recognized them, for she herself had written these simple words a few years ago in response to a whimsical greeting card. The card had featured the image of a stunning dragonfly, nicknamed "the darner" for its darning-needle-shaped body. In the moment, she allowed her own stirring message to parade through her mind

> "Lift off like the darner—in stillness—in breeze—
> and hover near ponds and mystical trees
> and quicken in realms of Holy Mystery
> Lift up on the wind—Transcendently be.
> Chorus
> Rising and lifting and soaring so free—
> Graced by the Lovelight—the essence of me."

Instead of getting frustrated with the insistent lyrical, interruption in her own headspace, Lyra realized the weight of the moment too. *Perhaps the Holiness of the previous Moment is still with me, and, maybe it is still nudging me, through the simple lyrics of the song, which I wrote so long ago?* She stopped trying to consciously control her headspace. She leaned back on the rock, in silence for a few moments. It felt right. It felt good. Her eyes were closed. She was peaceful.

A short time passed. With her eyes still closed, she could concentrate on what was arising within her. She was alive inside with wonder and with sensing. She became one in spirit with her pretty wilderness pond.

Lyra's mind started to wander. It was fluttering and flitting about. The French word for dragonfly, *Libellule*, came to mind. Then, the Spanish word for butterfly, *Mariposa*, wove itself through the threads of her thinking.

Then the word, *azure*, graced her flight of words. *Aloft. Alighting. Grace. Presence. Featherweight. Peaceful. Messenger. Transformation.* These words danced in her consciousness, intensifying Lyra's present feel-good-ful-ness, which was flowing freely throughout her whole being. She sighed mystically. *Oh, Libellule of loveliness. Oh Mariposa of magnificence, Oh allure of Azure, I reach for you, I sing to you! Let's dance and sing—Let our hearts take wing!*

Then, with her eyes still closed, Lyra slowly and surely, tuned into something beautiful. She couldn't say what was going on, only that it was beautiful. She saw no vivid images. She heard nothing. She felt no change in the movement of the air around her. But still, she marveled at the beauty. She didn't want this feeling to disappear and she knew it would, just like the Holy Moment simply came and went a few minutes ago. She thought about opening her eyes and then resisted. The urge to open her eyes became stronger, she still held back. *Why on earth am I causing myself all this tension and strife by choosing to keep my eyes closed? Just open your eyes old girl and see what happens!*

And then, it happened. It was unexpected and welcomed and soooooooo indescribably exquisite, all in the simple opening of her eyes.

Awe and Wonder and Delight

A magnificent dragonfly had come to Lyra, alighting on her left knee. It was actually looking upward and facing Lyra when she opened her eyes. Lyra was not frightened, or caught off guard at all. She simply gazed upon this iridescent queen of the pond, and she soaked in all the awe and wonder and joy of the moment.

A discernible aura of peace had encircled Lyra and the dragonfly. Any onlooker would have recounted seeing an emotive and tiny Aurora Borealis suspended like a misty cloud of light dancing around them. This awesome light-cloud was rising up from within them. But there were no onlookers.

Perhaps then, this little dragonfly is the source of that incredible beauty that I tuned into, just a few moments ago, while my eyes were closed? Perhaps, I'm simply attuning to my own spiritual senses, which are in turbulent overdrive, churning and overflowing in response to my oversized pond experience, here and now? Hmmmmm . . . .

Lyra delighted in this unhurried, unscheduled time. For a few moments, she focused exclusively on the delicate dragonfly wings. They were fine, yet they were powerful enough to be able to lift the unassuming winged queen upward against the perpetual pull of Mother Earth's gravity. They could lift her up into the air, to hover, to explore, to seek food, and to dart quickly out of danger.

She continued to gaze. She mused on the exquisite coloring of the whole creature. Iridescence everywhere. The glinting lavender, silver, gold, teal, rose, copper, and emerald lights of the moving wings, were absolutely mesmerizing. Breathtaking. Creation's natural wonder. The wings gave off an intermittent, soft fiery glow in the surrounding forest air. Dreamlike. Purely poetic.

Gazing deeper, she did not let any more thoughts enter her mind. She became profoundly still and silent. She felt honored that this awesome gift of Creation had chosen to linger with her for so long. Time flowed on. The speed of time passage meant nothing to her, right there, right then.

Something big is happening in my midst. I can feel it and I welcome it. I am truly blessed to be communing so intimately and so intensely with the dragonfly. Lyra knew all about suspension of disbelief, a tool used in imaginative and evocative writing. Little did she know, that her own personal limits of disbelief were about to be radically suspended in this perfectly poetic picture by the pond!

The Conversation Begins

"Hello Lyra!" said the dragonfly. "My name is Zoli! I've been waiting to meet you for a really long time!" Strangely enough, Lyra was not unnerved. She took this unique salutation totally in stride and she didn't miss her cue.

"Hello Zoli! How nice to meet you! I feel like I have been called to meet you here, by the still waters! And how very interesting that you have called me by my name! I must say that you are a wholesomely beautiful being! Your beauty is deeper than your looks and I can feel your beautiful presence all around me. Are all dragonflies capable of sharing their beauty in such tangible and intangible ways?"

"Yes and no" said Zoli. "Being open to, and feeling the grace of our presence, is more of a reflection of the human's abilities and not that of our own intrinsic powers. If a human is open, it makes a great difference in their life experiences—but more about this later. Right now I want to let you know that we already know each other in a very unique way. We know each other rather intimately."

Zoli continued "You wrote a mystical song about me, or maybe it was about God. You wrote it after I alighted upon you in the woods in the Springtime, when I remained with you, at length. Yours was contemplative delight and personal transcendence. Mine was the joy of our shared Light. Ours was indeed, a Holy Moment.

"After our encounter, you described a perfect peace that had suffused your very soul, a peace that you believe, came from me. You titled your song "One Holy Moment," and you set your impassioned lyrics to some very popular, secular melodies. The first four lines are sung to "You Raise Me Up" and the last four lines are the final strains of "Oh Danny Boy." You ingeniously created a crossover melody!" Lyra nodded, fondly remembering.

Zoli paused deliberately and sighed before posing her next barrage of questions. "Do you remember experiencing an absolute openness of your whole person—a lightness of your very being—as you wrote your lyrics?"

Lyra said "Yes! That was special."

Zoli asked "Do you remember your wide-eyed gaze when I first graced you with my presence?"

Lyra said with excitement "Yes, for sure! I remember I couldn't take my eyes off of you!"

"Do you recall seeing more intently—more richly—in those special moments? Can you open your eyes now, to *all* that you saw back then, in your Holy Moment?"

Lyra knew this was a tougher query. "There's some weight to this question Zoli, and I know that if I spend just a few moments, all the details of our time together will come flooding back to me. Ours were memorable moments, for sure. I titled my song "One Holy Moment" for good reason!" Lyra embraced this question, allowing it to take on vibrant colors and form in her mind.

Zoli extrapolated in her her questioning "Can you tap into that overwhelming sense of spaciousness, and expansiveness, that you sensed back then? Can you feel—can you revisit—our moments of integral interconnectedness? Can you bring all of those feelings forward into your being—and into your consciousness—into your now?"

Lyra was enchanted. "Zoli, I live in a village life setting, and I am well acquainted with the busy-ness of the real world and also in contrast, with the pure delights of my natural world experiences. I love to retreat into my times of spaciousness and expansiveness and interconnectedness. And I especially remember all of those feelings, and that blessed mindset, when I was with you—when I wrote that song."

"You Lyra, have sung with gooseflesh passion, oftentimes, about that special Holy Moment. May I remind you now, of your own song lyrics?" And Zoli sang out prayerfully, with poise and with passion:

"In ev'ry life there is a thirst and hunger
Each fervent heart seeks solace from life's trial
When I was still, just ling'ring in the sunshine
I prayed you'd sojourn there with me awhile.
Then you alighted sparkling and ablazing
Oh how I blushed resplendent in your Light
My restless heart transcended in the Lovelight
My weary soul found comfort in your Light!"

Lyra was quiet for a moment. Of course she recalled writing these lyrics. She treasured every single word! They were dear to her heart. She remembered quite distinctly, the draw of the spellbinding Holiness of that once-upon-a-springtime moment, while in the presence of that beautiful dragonfly—while in the presence of Zoli—while in the presence of God.

And she delighted in knowing that that very same dragonfly was with her, there and then, communing with her at the pond. Life was good.

But Zoli is asking a much bigger question. Zoli just asked if I remembered noticing, my own whole-person openness, when I had originally composed these heartfelt words. Lyra lingered awhile in her musing, for she knew that this was becoming yet another sweet Holy Moment by the pond. Zoli's question needed time for it to be savored, and time for Lyra to fully unpack its depths. And it deserved her complete focus and the gift of her richly reflective powers.

OPEN YOUR EYES!

Zoli gave Lyra lots of time to ponder. When Zoli noted that Lyra was indeed lightening up from the depths of her thinking, Zoli prepared to speak again. Zoli sensed Lyra's rising readiness. In that moment she had a wee glimpse into Lyra's receptive mindfulness.

Zoli said "Lyra, I'm here to encourage you today. I'm here to share my wisdom and the wisdom of the ages with you. You are open and welcoming to your God and to all things spiritual. I feel that now is a good time to share with you, to lead you in your thinking, and to move you forward with grace and with mystery on your path. I will paint pictures for you, with painstaking detail and clarity too. Are you okay if we take this time together, to prepare to grow—to seek the spaciousness of spirit needed in the processing of a timely life-lesson?"

Lyra looked searchingly at Zoli. Warmly, she responded "Yes!"

Zoli began. "Please hold onto these words in your head. If you glean nothing else from my long-winded sessions, please move forward in tenacity, with these words lighting your path. Open your eyes to the possibility of always becoming more fully human. My key phrases are simply, 'open your eyes', and 'always becoming'. I have many small lessons to share with you, but for these two biggest lessons, I will be very direct and to the point."

Zoli gently continued, "For the little lessons, we can muse together and work through them, but I want to be sure that you are grasping the magnitude of my big lessons today. You have already recently been through a lengthy time of personal reflection and discernment about your identity. And you have done some really good work on your own! I am a dragonfly, and I am a cross-cultural symbol, almost a universal symbol, of many important things—formation and transformation, and transcendence—all of which can most certainly help you."

Lyra listened. She was hopeful, attentive, intrigued.

Zoli said, "But you yourself must prepare. You must do the work. You must unlock your eyes to see more clearly. You must find the key and fling wide open the doors to your visual learning vault. Open the sluice gates and let the world of newness flood your vision, soak into your sight, and bathe your naked visual reality. Openness to new thinking, new information, new seeing, new perspectives, new paradigms, new colored lenses, new pathways—new new new new new!!! Intentionally open your eyes all around you 360 degrees—not just once in a while, but forevermore. Have 'open eyes' in all your approaches in life. Look at my eyes! Look at my own giant compound eyes. They are a living metaphor for 360 degree vision. You too can accomplish the art of this invaluable vision, simply by committing to try 360 vision, all the time, in all you do."

Zoli spoke ever so slowly and softly. Zoli went on in her delicate, assertive approach, "Open your eyes to the reality, and to the promise, of the living faith. Your friend John in Newfoundland, in the 1980s, fully and completely embodied the term—living faith. You witnessed daily through him, faith-based integrity, conviction, and human loving-kindness. He fortuitously planted the seeds, and opened your eyes to an amazing faith journey awaiting you, if only you too would live out your life in the wonders of the living faith. His personal example in his scripturally grounded ways was a turning point in your then-emerging faith journey. And this led you on your own transformative path in the living faith. Thanks be, for your friend John!"

"Yes, Zoli" Lyra added. "John was, not by design, my very first spiritual formation mentor way back then. He incidentally taught me things about living my faith—he opened my eyes to the wonders of a living faith, which I've never forgotten. I don't think he even knew the effects that his faith-based living had, and would have, on me over the years. I am grateful for John."

Zoli still had more to say. Quietly impassioned, she said "Open your eyes to see the real you. Open wider to see all of your God-given gifts and your talents and your blessings, your rock solid faith, and the incredible depths of your very own Celtic ancestral heritage. Come with your eyes wide open to see a very new and emerging version of you—to appreciate your current and newly realized identity. And try something new! Open the eyes of your heart! See where this will take you! You'll be amazed at what the heart can see and what the heart knows about compassion, respect, and reverence. What it knows about the Sacred and so much more." Lyra's eyes were wide open. She was ready to rise up to Zoli's call.

Zoli raised her voice just a little. "And then, for some amazing fine tuning of the new you, take the words of my smaller lessons—formation, transformation, and transcendence—and take them into your life and make them real. Make them come alive. Use them to open your eyes to the wonder and to the possibilities of not only who you are, but who you can become! Put yourself in the driver's seat and get on the road to opening your eyes to every possible version of you. This willful wide-eyed openness is truly life altering, life giving, and life blessing."

Lyra tilted her head, almost quizzically, as if she were trying to see from a different angle—to learn more through her new wide-angle vision.

Zoli raised and lowered her wings slowly, gracefully. "Soon, you'll want to ponder two more wonderful concepts and see how they resonate with you. The two unique words are simply, *being and becoming*. We often get stuck *on being something*, which is okay, but it can be self-limiting and stagnating. Once you've truly opened your eyes to *becoming more*, through intentional personal and spiritual formation, transformation, and transcendence, then you are well on the road to being more fully human, even to becoming most fully human. Your own identity will begin to evolve and emerge most clearly.

"Forgive me Lyra, if my words are beginning to sound intense. There is depth to what I am saying. I hope you're okay hearing all of this, out here in the forest on your leisurely walk!"

"Zoli, I'm drawn to your every word. Please, continue painting your pictures so I can learn more!"

Zoli looked relieved. She began again "You will want to come to a full awareness and understanding of your desire to realize your own humanity, and your desire to actualize your own humanity. Your very own journey toward becoming most human will, in a sense, be your ultimate journey into self-actualization—in all planes, in all realms, in all spheres. Becoming most fully human doesn't mean becoming extraordinary, outstanding, phenomenal, or even superhuman. Rather, it is truly the art and the passion of becoming deeply, intensely, human. This sounds a bit heavy, but it is easy with a receptive spirit, with eyes wide open." Lyra nodded in agreement.

Zoli spoke with increasing passion. "Research psychologists and transformation therapists tell us that becoming, is fluid. Becoming is dynamic. Becoming is transcendent. Becoming is a dynamic journey of transcendence. Hold this in your heart. Open the eyes of your heart to see this—to recognize this. Soon, you'll come to feel and to know that you are seeing with the eyes of your heart. You will actually see, feel and know, that you are becoming.

"This is a lot of work and it won't be accomplished in a single day or a week. But with great personal determination, fortitude, and conviction, open eyes will open many doors on your pathway to becoming. It's that simple."

Resistance

Zoli stopped for a moment to allow all of her words to float in the luminous airspace around Lyra and then for them to be absorbed by the spongy cells of her soulful being. There was a look in Lyra's eyes that encouraged Zoli. It was a look of hunger and thirst. The wheels were turning in Lyra's head as she was voraciously processing the breadth and the depth of the dragonfly's lesson.

But sadly, Zoli saw something else too. In Lyra's eyes, she saw physical micro-expressions—memories or expressions of hurt, and angst, and possibly fear. For a millisecond, Zoli actually saw a fleeting hopelessness in Lyra's soft sage green eyes. Zoli gave Lyra the space and time she needed to collect her emotions and to share them if she felt free to do so.

And Lyra opened her heart. "Zoli, I'm feeling somewhat resistive to part of your lesson, and I think I know why. I struggled a long time ago with 'intentional being and becoming.' Due to my own sister's medically complex health and her physical limitations, she struggled in school and in sports, and her shyness made it tough for her to make lasting friendships. And I was quite the opposite.

"My own mom one day, flat out asked me as a young teenager, to just be kind and considerate and sensitive to my older sister's limited life. She said, 'Instead of always being "someone" or becoming "something", just try being "you". Stop getting in your sister's face by doing all the things she cannot do.'"

Well, if words could literally crush, Lyra's spirit could be likened, in that moment long ago, to a flat pancake, or a fine crepe, or even finer still, to a singleton phyllo pastry sheet. Lyra groaned, "I'll never forget the flail and the lash, and the fiery licking of her cold hard words on my spirit. Mom then said 'Being the best,' 'becoming somebody,' and 'becoming something more' are all so highly over-rated. And it's a lot of hard work, always focusing on getting ahead and being more. Just be satisfied with being your own person and with being your own simple self. Your big sister, BJ, would like that.'

"Well, as much as I understood what my mom was saying for my sister's sake, I felt in that moment that my mom didn't really know my heart, and she certainly didn't get who I really was. I felt grossly misunderstood. I was smart and so very athletic and ultra-creative. I was an achiever, and I was highly motivated to get a post-secondary education that would lead to a challenging and interesting career. My mom's words felt like the sludgy mucky weight of tidal river mudflats holding me down, sinking me and sucking me down. I was suddenly suffocating. I felt like a big dark dome had been intentionally plunked down over top of me, limiting the perimeter of my personhood. I had an inferno of anger raging inside of me. And worst of all, I felt the pain and the searing of a molten metal blade stabbing into my back, right through to my heart. Out of my own well-conditioned and dutiful respect for my mom, I held my tongue, and squelched my angry words. I obviously had no place there and then, to vent my fire or its fumes. I intentionally repressed my anger, because it was just easier than dealing with it. I learned to talk to God in prayer. And that helped me a lot.

"So Zoli, needless to say, it was many, many years before I even allowed myself to contemplate 'my being,' let alone 'my becoming.' I was truly conflicted. I wanted to honor my mom's wishes, to simply be me. But, I also knew that there was a whole wonderful world out there, where I could learn and grow—and become. I wanted to know and to discover who I really was. I wanted to know my role, my purpose in life.

"Despite all of my clashing feelings, I was able to move on. I did move on, and I had a wonderful education and career in both Emergency Nursing and in Parish Nursing Ministry. I was able to use my gifts, my smarts, and my ever-expanding Health Sciences knowledge base, along with my deeply rooted faith, to give complete and compassionate care to all of my patients and their families. 'Whole-person health.' Body, mind, and spirit health.

"I hadn't gone into nursing for rewards, but I always felt richly rewarded throughout my nursing career. And, especially so, in the times when I knew in my heart that 'I had made a difference.' In its own way, my nursing career, and living the Compassionate Life, actually allowed me 'to become' the best version of me. It allowed me 'to become' more fully human, and to be more sensitive to the human condition. Despite my mom's negative and cautionary words, the Compassionate Life most surely gave me permission to live out a career-long journey of 'becoming more.'"

Roadblock

Tears then welled up in Lyra's eyes, as more dark memories cascaded into her consciousness. She looked directly at Zoli and blurted out, "My own sister hated me. I remember one afternoon when we were teenagers, BJ just let out all of her redheaded freckle-faced rage and she hollered out at me, at the top of her lungs "I hate you! I—HATE—YOU!!! Go away! Get away from me. You're a constant reminder of all the things I cannot do and cannot be! I HATE YOU!!!"

"Her words stunned me. They stung. And they reverberated loudly, like the clanging and chaotic echoes of a falling stack of metal pots and pans. She might as well have spat on me. My spirit and my innermost me completely collapsed. Her hatred for me literally stopped me in my tracks, like a massive rock-slide roadblock to my entire future. I felt like I couldn't move forward at all—not even a measly millimeter forward—without hurting my sister."

Lyra's floodgates were opened wide and she sobbed, releasing a lifetime of hurting and grief, into her gushing salty tears. "I know deep down in my heart that she didn't hate me forever. It was only in the heat of the moment, but BJ could not unsay those damaging and hateful words. Never. Ever. BJ's life was so restricted by her illness and by her physical limitations. She always had to work really hard just to get through each day. Every day for her was just more work. BJ died way too young at age 38. We all miss her dearly."

Lyra went on "But for sure, BJ left her mark on my life. A really good mark for that matter. Underneath BJ's shy persona, was a deep well of inner wisdom. She had an insight into humanity that was not schooled, rather, it was inborn. And it was uniquely hers. She saw into people's souls, and she understood their hearts.

"I was with her one day at an arts and crafts fair, and she bought a small iron frying pan, with painted pink and white flowers on the bottom and sides and a beautiful hand written message that read, 'Happiness is Homemade.' These words touched her heart. They resonated deeply in BJ's soul. BJ had actually lived out those very words. They soon became her daily mantra. Her eyes were open wide to glass-half-full-living. She had such an inner strength and a fervent resolve, to count her blessings in every day, no matter what—and to be happy, no matter what.

"BJ had veritably grown out of her childhood angst of discontent, desire and want, and she had become contented with herself and with her current life and her lifestyle. She was peaceful. She was happy. She had an insight into humanity that would eventually define her very being.

"In her grace and maturity, she was truly grateful for all that she did have. In her young adult, wise-beyond-her-years outlook, she did not let what she didn't have, or couldn't have, or couldn't do, get the better of her anymore. Despite all of her limitations, and her still living at home for thirty-eight years with our parents, she had enough life experience to know, that no one can make you happy but you, yourself. Happiness is indeed homemade.

"To this day, I still have that pretty frying pan hanging on my kitchen backsplash, as an ongoing reminder of and a tribute to my sister's inner strength and wisdom. My dear sister, is now the redheaded angel, the sage soul of the heavens. Her insights into humanity will rest gently on my heart, forever."

Raw Regret

BJ had also been sweetly sensitive with sisterly concern through the years, to Lyra's sadness over her own ticking biological clock. BJ knew deep down, that Lyra yearned to mother a child and that the sun was slowly setting on her fertile years. BJ had also secretly longed to be an Auntie to Lyra's children, as she knew in her own heart of hearts, that she also could never ever become a mom herself—a pregnancy would have been too risky for her, with her fragile and complicated health.

One day in the 1990s, BJ spoke plainly to Lyra, saying 'Maybe having a child is not in God's master plan for you, Lyra. Perhaps you need to trust in God's call on your life, whatever that may be. It's possible that you need to grieve your losses—in not being a mom—and move boldly in the direction that God is calling you. Is it possible, that you just cannot hear God's call, because you are living in sorrow, in regret—in want? Maybe down the road when you're healed and feeling more contented—after your grieving of your losses—you might be more open to symbolically birth something else in your life—something exquisitely meaningful that is arising from within you and waiting to be born. Maybe when you are finally able to hear God's plan, or God's call on your life, when you cast away all of your regrets and open yourself to God—maybe that's when you can bring something fresh and new and alive into this world. Hold the hope of new birth alive. Hold this hope, in your heart. Be open to a symbolic birthing, whatever that looks like, whatever that may be. Open your eyes and be fully open to the reality of symbolic birthing—as a very important part of your becoming.'

Back then, Lyra had keenly listened to BJ, to BJ's take on living a life without woe or regret. BJ was an old soul. A living saint. Most surely, she was the sage sibling. In those days, Lyra was totally devastated and crushed by the thoughts of never being—never becoming—a mom. She felt empty. Lost. Unfulfilled. Punished. Her self-worth sank slowly and desperately and deeply. Her darkness would creep constantly into her consciousness, shrouding and clouding her ways and her days. She really didn't like her lackluster living, languishing in the lows of life—living lost—living in loss. She couldn't—and didn't—articulate this then, but she knew she didn't like living without hope, without Light.

Oftentimes, she'd get a timely, tsunami-sized wave of a reality check. With no husband or a partner even on her visible horizon while she was nearing forty—and with her long hours in arduous shift work at the hospital, she knew in her heart that bringing a child into her solitary life was probably asking for trouble. Nonetheless, she still ached with emptiness. She still dearly longed to be a mom. She longed to bring new life and new love into her world and into her heart.

She had confided in BJ in that moment, way back then. Hopes and dreams—and 'what-ifs' and 'if-onlys'—arose from her heart and from the darkest depths of her soul. Her words turned into tears. Torrents and tidal waves of tears. BJ's responsive hug was a quiet, knowing embrace, a shoulder to sink into, a safe shelter in the wilderness of Lyra's Saharan storm.

"Zoli, I was so drawn to BJ's sagacious wisdom. But, it was years and years and years before I could really let go, before I could completely trust in God's leading, before I could intentionally open myself to birthing something else—to bearing up something phenomenally pithy and powerful from deep down within—something that would be life-changing for me down the road. Something that, when born, would help me to shine—to shine brightly."

Unspoken Lament

Out of the blue, Lyra had a new, not-so-nice, physical sensation percolating within her depths. It became notably stronger, then all-encompassing. She felt like she was plummeting, free-falling, accelerating—being pulled down and away against her will. Her emotions were rapidly descending in the moment, to a dank, dark place. A lightless place. Waves of shame and ineptitude washed over her, dashing her spirit. She felt worthless, unworthy, undesirable. She felt suddenly lost, disconnected, ever so briefly. She was entering into a memory of a place in time—an unspeakably hollow place— a loathsome and painful place.

Then and there, she didn't let on to Zoli what she was thinking. She knew from past experience, that there were 'things' that you just do not talk about, 'things' that you do not openly share with anyone, ever. 'Things' that were too dark to name, too deep to burden friends and family with, and too frightening to actually put into words. 'Things' that, if spoken out loud, would proclaim her obvious vulnerability, showcase her inherent weakness, and cause her to appear 'less than' in others' eyes. They might even pity her.

So she withheld her words. She did not want Zoli to see how truly vulnerable she was. Lyra wanted Zoli to still value her.

Lyra had recently learned some refreshing words from a popular podcast speaker. Their message was enlightening and hope-rendering. Lyra had learned that being vulnerable—showing vulnerability—does not, in effect, make you weak. Rather, it was quite the opposite. Being vulnerable, naming your vulnerability, and sitting with your vulnerability, are all indeed first steps—strong first steps—in healing, in transformative thinking, in moving forward—in becoming a strong self once again. She chose to cling to that message—to find strength in that memorable message—in the moment by the pond with Zoli.

In the past, Lyra had made only one exception in sharing her vulnerability story—her angst. She had voiced her unspoken lament to God in prayer, repeatedly, ever since her young adult days. As much as she truly enjoyed being single and free—free to explore her world, her faith, her dreams, her passions—all of this came with one big drawback. Lyra's lament. She had no life-partner and therefore no promise of love-for-life. She so needed to love, and be loved. She wanted to be intimately known, body, mind and soul. She yearned to have a soul mate, a husband, a love who would know her inside and out and, who would accept her and cherish her for who she truly was. Someone who would not only treasure but celebrate, her gifts. Someone who would choose to help her to work through her faults and her shortcomings. Someone who understood her and who would help her evolve and grow on her terms. Someone who would delight in sharing together all that life and love could bring, in joy and in laughter, in sorrow and in loss.

For Lyra, this love, this accepting and helping spirit, this committed relationship, would be life changing and life blessing. At least, she dreamed that it could be. Longer, deeper, stronger, higher, were words describing dimensions of love. Enduring love. Unconditional love. A bonding love that would withstand all the tests of time. A love that knew no limits. Lyra aspired to this love. In its absence, she felt incomplete—unfulfilled, undesirable, unwanted and unloved—unlovable. So many un-words. So much un. Lyra's lament of un.

Lyra would have liked nothing more than to live out the rest of her days, being known, loved, and understood. She wanted—she needed—to be cherished. She longed for a love that would complete her and make her whole. She yearned. She hoped. She prayed. God had heard her every lament, her every prayer, her every word. And Lyra knew this. She chose to keep her darkest lament private from her world, sharing it with no one, but with God.

God is a great listener. All I have to do is call out to God, and he is there, with me in prayer. Any season, any reason, he is there. And, I believe that prayer changes things. Prayer changes me, for sure. Being known, loved and understood by God—being in an intimate relationship in my prayer-life with God—is a grand gift in itself. Divine love is blessed love. But, I want more. I pray for more. I need to be loved. Loved by a man, fully, wholly, completely— unconditionally. I want to experience all of the wonders of selfless, authentic love. And I want to return this love. What if I'm never loved? What if I'll al- ways be alone? What if no one ever, truly, knows me—knows my heart? Yes, I am contented with my current free-spirited, unattached life. But, I ache for—I hunger and thirst for—love. Beautiful, reciprocal, human love. Lyra smiled warmly, having finished her impassioned interior monologue. Loads lifted. Released.

More

Zoli had given Lyra the time and space she needed to reflect in silence. She had felt the fiery intensity of Lyra's raw emotions. And then Zoli noticed something else. Zoli felt arising within herself a freshness in hopefulness, a blossoming positive energy, and a billowing notion of Lyra feeling freed after having openly shared some of her darker emotions and memories.

Zoli nodded slowly, knowingly, and patiently.

Then Lyra suddenly recalled something else that her sister had in- nately known. It was like BJ had an inner fount of spiritual intuition. She would often interject in an ordinary conversation, with words of pure and simple truth.

Lyra said "And one day after church, BJ asked me 'Do you ever feel like you are more, with God?'" Lyra became notably pensive, as she chose her words carefully. It was almost like she was showcasing the grand reveal of a timeless museum treasure.

Lyra continued to unfold the words of her heart. "I was only in my twenties back then, and I was still a long way away from being a spiritually- grounded soul. When BJ put that question out to me, it felt like she was unlocking something in me. Opening something. Opening my eyes.

"That very question became a doorway, or a threshold into my Contemplative Life. It was a very big question, and it was one that I would return to many more times over the years."

Zoli's eyes glinted powerfully, in the moment. Lyra's tangential backstory was intriguing her.

Lyra went on "And, my answer through the years would also come to evolve, along with my own expansive broadening on my spiritual formation journey. At that time, BJ had piped up and answered her own question and I chose to eagerly listen for the depths of her questioning mind—for the depths of her seeking soul." Lyra then quoted BJ, saying these words, adding her own lyric emphases

"**I** am more with God.
I **AM** more with God.
I am more **WITH GOD**.
I am **MORE** with God."

And with great conviction in her steady voice, BJ continued. "I am more alive and energized, knowing God is with me. I am more hopeful, enthusiastic and optimistic, with God. I am more content, more complete, and more whole, in the wonder of God's presence. I am more ready and willing, with the strength I have in God. I have a greater insight into myself and into my community and world and into humanity because God is walking the journey of life with me. I am simply more of everything that is good, with God. Do you feel this too? Have you ever tuned into simply 'being more with God'?"

Lyra continued "And my answer was simply 'I had never really thought about it, like that, in those words. BJ, you've given me a gift. It's not only something to think about, but, it is a way of thinking. A new perspective and framework for 'seeing me in my own life.' Thank you, BJ, for opening my eyes to such a contemplative way of seeing and being.'"

Affirmation

Over a bit of time, Zoli let a heavenly and healing silence hover in their pond haven of a meeting place. Zoli had given Lyra precious time and space to go deep, deeper. She had allowed Lyra's silent reflections to take her where they would, into the depths. Zoli had come into a fuller understanding of the fleeting micro-expressions she had witnessed earlier in

Lyra's eyes. Then Zoli and Lyra's eyes met for a few connecting seconds. Zoli saw that comfort, calm and conviction had settled into Lyra's countenance. No more visible signs of smoldering darkness or private personal pain. No more unsettling micro-expressions. Lyra looked more relaxed and ready.

"You've come a long way Lyra. You stayed true to yourself all these years, and you have become a strong woman for it. You know your own heart, and you know your own needs. You knew at a very young age that you were here on earth to do good works. Your eyes have literally been open for a lifetime already—open to perspective, nuance, wisdom and truth—open to see the highs and lows in relationship, joy and sorrow. And this has helped you to stay your course, to stay strong, and to see family, friends, and patients, through your perceptive eyes.

"I'm hoping that by now you have forgiven your sister, your mom, and yourself, for any perceived wrongfulness or misunderstood actions on all of your parts. Forgiveness truly sets you free."

Lyra nodded. "I have, for sure. And it felt good to just let it all go. I literally 'let go and let God' carry my burdens. 'For his yoke is easy and his burden is light.' My mom was a wonderful mom, despite our differing approaches to life. She had the difficult task of managing two daughters with vastly differing needs. She did her very best, and she did it all with love and devotion. She loved being our mom.

"And my sister's last words to me before she slipped into her coma and died—I will hold those precious words in my heart forever. She said 'Lyra, neither of us were bad sisters to each other. We were just two very different people, two very different people who knew how to share their love, no matter what. I love you, Lyra.'" Lyra paused for a moment, as her tender emotions were surfacing again. "Because of BJ, I see people. I know people. I get people. I became more human through knowing BJ, through seeing people and life, through her eyes."

Zoli continued delicately "Not all becoming is easy, or straightforward, or simple. I can tell that you already know this firsthand. Your emotions do speak for you. I simply want you to hold my words in your heart and to let the very real open-eyed you continue to emerge—continue to become.

"I want you to embrace an open-eyed, wide-eyed approach in the newness and freshness of all your daily living—360 degree vision. I want so very much for you, Lyra! Blessings to you Lyra, on your journey of becoming, in your identity seeking, and in your transformation into your newly envisioned you!"

On Becoming

Zoli said "I have more to share with you Lyra, if you're ready."

Lyra nodded, and replied "Wonderful Zoli! Anything you'd like to share, I'm ready to listen. So very ready."

Zoli moved along in her spirit of teaching. "Let's talk about transformation. Here we are in the wilderness, at the very edge of this newly expanded pond. On the surface, it appears calm and still and serene. But don't let it fool you! For under the pond surface is a whole different microcosm, even a macrocosm, depending on who is describing it! There may be some or many life-forms—tadpoles, snails, amoebae, larvae, algae, frogs, bullfrogs, reeds, weeds, lily pads, and much more.

"There are so many species of creatures and plants under the water and all of those life forms are not presently experiencing 'life as they have always known it.' For their quiet and still pond life had just recently been turned upside down. The water table had been extremely high when the weeklong rains came, causing the edges of the pond to extend out further into the forest bed. The pond neighborhood had unexpectedly grown. All pond life was in a bona fide tizzy! Everything was topsy-turvy. Underwater landmarks had changed and so had the underwater flows. The waters were murky. Species felt lost, rattled, unsure. Daily habitual routines were all disrupted.

"But still, life went on. And it still goes on. They seek food. They stay safe from predators. They even still make babies. They choose to enjoy life fully and to make the best of their changing world. They are not stagnating. They are becoming. Becoming more. Becoming fuller. Changing. Adapting. Transforming. Becoming most fully who they are.

"And Hey! Lyra! I'm a dragonfly and I personally faced great identity changes and went through many processes of transformation to become the very being that I am today! I once was an egg in the water, then a waterbound larva, then an aquatic nymph and naiad, and now look at me! I am regally and majestically dressed for living resplendently in the lofty air world—in the wind and in the breeze. Talk about the work of intentional transformation over time! Talk about taking time—it took me five years underwater to become more fully me, as an integral creature of my ever-changing microcosmic world. I am one with the Light of my world. Life is good."

Zoli had been intently studying Lyra's face during her lesson. Lyra's whole demeanor was indeed warm, and truly receptive, and of all things, open! Zoli could see that Lyra was encouraged by her words, no longer leery, resistive and negative, but truly open and welcoming of her timely words of wisdom. Zoli knew that Lyra had turned the corner in her growing appreciation of both 'being and becoming'.

Lyra and Zoli lingered together, Lyra seated on the rock with her left leg dangling in the ankle-deep water. Zoli was comfortably grounded on Lyra's left knee. Any passerby would have questioned the reality of this scene—an eloquent dragonfly speaking to a humble human on a massive rock settee by a rarefied pond, basking in the softly-filtered, sparkling Light of their souls? *La Demoiselle et la Lumière de Dieu?* But, there were no passersby. Only two souls engaging intimately and intellectually as One, in the Light.

The Word of God

In Real Time—In Prayer

Beloved,
I have called you by your name, you are mine.
When you walk through the waters, I will be with you,
and through the rivers, they shall not overwhelm you.
When you walk through the fire you shall not be burned,
and the flames will not consume you.
I will be with you, My Beloved. Amen.

LESSON TWO

Across the Universal Sky
Meet Yala—the Celtic Raven

Above me drifts the indigo sky—a rich auroral dome—
Expansive host of wisdom—truth—Contemplatives 'at home'.
Arising in the limitless space—the grand ethereal muse—
A feast of knowledge, insight, grace—Prodigious worldly views.

Sage or Sacred?

Lyra sighed. Earlier this morning she had ventured out on a nature walk in the forest and had only gone as far as the pond where she had tarried in conversation with Zoli, the informative dragonfly. She was so magnetically drawn to this tiny, seemingly supernal being. Zoli related to her, as an astute teacher would to an exemplary pupil. Lyra's mind was working overtime, trying to absorb all of the special lessons, big and small.

It was around 11:00 a.m. Time to move on with purpose. Her newfound pearls of wisdom would have to be stored in her memory—in the dark vault of her prefrontal cortex—for the time being, until she could take her time to reflect more deeply through them. She looked forward to pondering them, and bringing them into her comfort zone, into her reality, and into the Light.

She put on her hiking shoes and laced them securely. Wanting to be hands-free as she walked, she donned her summer-weight cardigan. She said "Zoli, this has been a wonderful time in the pond neighborhood, and a wonderful opportunity for me to meet you, my pond neighbor—to meet you again! It has been a chance for me to slow right down and listen deeply, in earnest. To listen well.

"Thank you so much for being my pond neighbor and for taking all of this time with me! You seem to know so much about the human condition and some very specific strategies to help out me personally. Thanks for taking a genuine interest in my journey and for so kindly helping me along the way!"

"Lyra, my friend, this was my pleasure! You are not alone in your coddiwompling journey to find yourself, identify yourself, and reinvent yourself, using all of your God-given gifts. Many others are walking this very same road with you, in their own parts of the world. They share your same purposefulness, in their own headspace and spiritual musings, in their own quests and journeys.

"You learned your lesson well this morning about opening your eyes. I'm sure you'll meet many sages along your journey—teachers, advocates, messengers and more. All of whom will ask you to open yourself in some new and special ways in order to hear and to comprehend, and embody, their equally important messages."

It was time for Lyra to ask the really big question that lay across her heart. "You are such a knowing creature, Zoli! Who are you, that you know so much about all of life—so intuitively and in so much vivid detail?"

Zoli paused with intent. She then spoke with clearly chosen words. "Lyra, I am a Celtic mystical being. I transformed from my life in the dark deep waters to a life in the Light and the wind. I have intrinsic transcendent powers and my pond neighbors recognize my transcendent soul. I have ancient worldly knowledge, and intuitions, which emanate from deep within me.

"I attune deeply to the mysteries of energy, matter, space and time—to of all life in my midst. Woven into my essence are the light-bearing threads of love, peace, and respect for all of Creation. I am born of Holiness and so are you. I delight in "seeing" the Sacred in you, and in all life. Does any of this help you to understand me, in this moment, here and now?"

Lyra had a sweet and contented look on her face. She wished she could hug Zoli. Instead, and with intent, she laid down her left index finger on her left thigh, directly in front of Zoli's face. Zoli accepted the invitation and gently lifted herself up onto Lyra's finger, using her graceful wings. Lyra then raised Zoli up to eye level. She gazed intensely into Zoli's oversized compound eyes and gave her a demure and deep nod of gratitude.

As Lyra stood up from her rocky pond-view bench, Zoli was aloft and hovering, moving onward in the Light. In the stillness of the moment, Lyra stood by the pond and prayed out loud with her eyes wide open and her palms lifted upward to her God.

> "Thank you for voices that my ears can hear.
> Thank you for lessons that I hold so dear.
> Thank you for opening my eyes to the Light—
> Thanks for your presence in Holy Lovelight. Amen."

Not a day goes by without Lyra offering her responsive prayers. It was her spontaneous way. It was her heartfelt antiphon. It was her gift.

Grace and Prayer

Trekking on, Lyra recalled a small square art print, a wrapped canvas, which hung on the wall over her table on the north-side veranda. She could see it clearly from her veranda rocking chair. She had placed it there to use as a daily reminder to her of its simple life-forming words:

> "Grace is a state of heart—a state of being.
> Grace is a way of life!"

And her prayerful heart then prompted her to recall her very own formative catch phrase. She inwardly recited these engaging words, at the edge of the pond, near the edge of the forest. These words emerged from the reaches of her understanding and from her personal prayer-life experience:

> *Prayer is simply the "Posture of Presence"*
> *when you are fully and completely and intentionally and relationally*
> *present and receptive to the Sacred Ever-Presence*
> *in the moments and the mysteries in your own humble life—*
> *in your own true heart of grace.*

Her contemplative impulses were causing her to merge these two expressive thoughts into one compelling stand alone thought progression, as she reflected on her own prayer life. She spoke tentatively out loud, "A life of prayer—A life of grace—Presence in Ever-Presence." *Hmmmmm . . . .*

Contemplative Mindset

Lyra began to walk again on the path, away from the pond, following the trail, deep in thought. Over the last year, she had given herself to a great deal of study. She loved feeling solidly grounded with new knowledge. She loved the phrase "Knowledge is power." Knowing, made her feel strong.

During her retirement, Lyra had caught up on reading some contemplative authors' works (Benner, Berry, Brown-Taylor, Brown—Ghandi, Gorman, Gourley—Lawrence, Merton, Newell—Nouwen, Rohr, Sims—Vanier, Wagamese, Williamson).

She had traveled for weeks in Scotland, touring her ancestral regions of East Loch Lomond, in Buchanan Country. Then, she attended a retreat on the Isle of Iona where she communed with seekers and scholars of the Celtic Christian tradition. The Celtic Wisdom resonated with her.

She dove into her amassed collection of textbooks on Celtic history, wisdom and poetry. She had an insatiable hunger for learning. She was a starveling for truth and wisdom. Her quest for spiritual deeperlings, nuance, and fresh perspective consumed her and dominated her contemplative queries. She wanted to be shaped by her knowledge. Both academic and experiential, her readings were stirring, causing her to tingle in gooseflesh.

In her studies and discernment, Lyra was intuitively building a nest of new knowledge to ground her personhood. She took a course in spiritual direction and delighted in the extensive course reading list. She submitted multiple assignments to her mentor, Jan. These reflection papers showcased her ever-contemplative spirit. She had something worthwhile to say—lots to say—and she articulated this well in her written works.

She specifically remembered one paper. Her own written words flooded her mind as she walked. *Contemplation is both the intentional and incidental holding of space for many or single fragmented thoughts and allowing them to float, or to take on weight, or to dance in the light and the breeze, or to filter freely through time and space—transcending all boundaries perceived or real—and then the taking on of a sense of order, logic, and priority, and possibly emerging with more clarity and understanding, with metaphorical and lyrical and profound images in the heart and mind.*

Lyra then recalled a stirring session she'd had with her mentor just one year ago. Jan had been a trusted sounding board for Lyra as she explored her spiritual identity and purpose. On that particular day, she had said to Jan, "I need to come to clarity. My thoughts are random, and nebulous, and chaotic. I am truly grounded with God—my relational identities in him are *His*, *Beloved*, and *Called*. But there are other functional identities that call to me too, like, Poet, Writer, Contemplative, Mystic, and Sage. Since I am not known in the literary world as yet—I am not a published author—I feel that my claiming these identities as my own seems lofty, pretentious, and larger than me. I am conflicted. I am at a great divide in the grand river of life. Many watercourses to follow. Many choices to make. I want to know more of me—the truest me."

Jan had simply listened to Lyra, not saying—not interjecting—anything that would interrupt Lyra's train of thought. Jan could see—she could feel arising in herself—that Lyra was poised on a brink of self-revelation, of self-identity, of self-knowing. Jan intuited that it was just a matter of time before Lyra would articulate her new identity. She would name her new being and becoming. Jan knew that Lyra, through her own contemplative labors, would soon give birth to her new identity.

Lyra was almost there when she said to Jan "For years I have certainly been a closet poet, lyricist, and song writer. The words of this modern-day prophet won't be written on subway walls, or in blaring blogs. No. These words, my words, need to be read widely. In churches. In schools. At home. In print media. In books. I can share the Celtic Wisdom. My words can teach, encourage, and heal. My words can reach, gather, and hold. My words can shine Light—shine brightly. I do believe in the power of my words. And now, my humble inner me needs to step out of my comfort zone and get my work published. Get my work out there. The time is now."

Lyra, on the path in the woods, smiled as she recalled her time with Jan. It had been an amazing experience to share the complexities of her identity journey with someone who cared enough to listen deeply and truly hear her words. Jan's heart heard Lyra's. Lyra's heart was grateful.

Lyra's mind moved forward, onward, to two more words upon which she had recently reflected. "Spaciousness" and "expansiveness". Both, in her mindful pursuits, were words that felt good to her, and they were relevant in describing the scope of her thinking and the depth of her queries and the vastness of her present mind.

Having both a wholesome spaciousness of my being and an ever-present expansiveness of my mindset simply allows me to enter into my profoundly contemplative realms. My own personal degree of spaciousness and expansiveness, could easily lead me to increased receptivity—to greater depths of my perceptions. They could tromp on and stomp on any of my judgmental or preconceived notions of any subject matter at hand.

There and then on the forest trail beyond the pond, Lyra tuned in to her own growing sense of spaciousness of her whole being and to the willing expansiveness of her current mindset. Her whole person, body mind and spirit, was in a state of readiness—of mindfulness—of openness. She felt good.

Little did Lyra know that her life, her lens, her love, her passions, and her muse were about to take a grand mystical journey through all she could possibly know, from the center to the edge, and back again. Like the rivershore welcoming the running waves with enthusiastic open arms, Lyra's faith gathered in and collected itself, gracing itself in perseverance and in perpetuity. Her faith and her spiritual formation—like the waters—shimmered in the Light.

The Veil

Lyra's vision suddenly changed. She stopped in her tracks on the trail. She brought her hands up to her eyes to rub them ever so gently. Upon opening her eyes, she still wasn't sure of what she was seeing or what was happening.

Right there in front of her, in the freshness of the forest, was a grand semblance of sparkle, a translucent film, a vertical veil of Light that veritably dulled all of the scenery behind it. It hovered, shimmering—billowing forth from heaven to earth. It almost seemed to be fluid—flowing, dynamic, in the stillness of time. In sweet serene silence, it was colorful, comforting, and completing. It was at once poetic, and real. It was not in the least bit frightening or intimidating. Rather, it was welcoming, and beckoning. In the wide-open spaciousness and expansiveness of her present being, Lyra was witnessing a Light-bearing phenomenon, a moment of Light, most surely unlike any other.

It was massive, directly in front of her on the path, in the open-spaced gnarly-treed woods. Remaining standing before the ethereal veil, she was awed by its enormity, intrigued by its Presence and drawn to commune with it. She was compelled to be part of it, whatever it was.

She stepped forward. Closer. She took a second step. A third step brought her close enough to reach out and touch the vibrant veil. To her surprise, there was no tactile sensation. Her hand touched nothingness. Absolute nothingness. She leaned forward and realized that her hand could go right through the veil, into the Light.

She listened intently with her ears, with her heart, and with her faith. She felt called to step through the sparkling spectacle, to the other side.

Time stopped. Lyra had traversed into the mystery of the moment. She had crossed over a threshold, through the Light, to a state of being. She had stepped into a Presence, an aura of the Divine. There was no sound, but silence. There was no time, but the present. There was nothing but Lyra's mystical call into the vastness of her now.

Lyra waved aside her cloud of bewilderment and took on a cloak of grace. She cast away all of her concerns and became daringly disinhibited. Lyra did not speak. Nor did she question. She just wanted this moment to be allowed to unfold in its own mystery. In the silence, she felt welcomed. In the Light, she felt immersed. She felt at home.

Her unruly mop of shimmering ringlets morphed into an opalescent halo, glistening with a Light all of its own. She could not see the halo, but she could feel the warmth of its Light. Her fair freckles dawned and danced in the Light. Her eyes became gently luminous, glowing from a Light within. Her smile curled, waxing in awe and in wonderment. No songs were ringing out. No birds were singing out. Not even the drone of the ancient mystical om was on her spiritual radar. Her heart slowed. Her breathing slowed. She became One in the veil—One in the Light.

Lyra knew that this was a Holy Moment, for she sensed that God was fully present to her. Had she just entered into a veritable spiritual realm, or did it exist only in her own consciousness? Was this veiled visual phenomenon actually real or was it a colorful construct of her spacious subconscious? Or, just maybe, was it the purely poetic wanderings of her limitless imagination?

Lyra stopped her incessant questioning. This was all too extraordinary to even try to qualify, or quantify, with words, or poetry, or story. This— whatever this was—was Holy.

And then, in wonderment, she heard it! Her ears and her whole person, received the gift—the gift of a message through the veil, and through the Light. A nearby voice was speaking softly, earnestly, from within the sparkle of the veil. The voice was close by, up close and personal. It was intimately, palpably near.

She heard the gentle voice say "*Ephphatha*! Lyra, *Ephphatha*!" She knew that God was speaking to her. And she understood, from her long-ago Bible Study classes, the ancient Aramaic word to mean, "Be opened!"

She bowed her head and closed her eyes and entered into a silent prayer. Her heart was overwhelmed, humbled. Gratitude overflowed. Lyra inwardly came alive, in reverence, in joy, in peace. *God has come to me! God is present to me! God is speaking to me and calling me by my name. God is encouraging me.* She closed her silent prayer with these words:

> *God of all Being, God of all Mystery, God of Light and Love,*
> *Thanks be, for You are here, with me.*
> *I am open, indeed. Amen.*

Lyra paused in the finest silken tulle of silence, and she slowly opened her eyes. No fiery sparkle. No glistening organza. No thinnest gossamer. No more luminous voluminous veil. To her dismay, all she could see in front of her was the forest, the path, and the way forward. Nonetheless, she stood there, feeling full in her heart, full in her soul—full of Light in her very being.

Lyra took one long slow breath in. She closed her eyes as she breathed out. God was still with her. She opened her eyes and moved onward on the trail.

The deciduous forest path was wide and dry, thankfully. Lyra had walked this path many many times before over her forty years of living by the river. Some of the cleared trails had been there since the early settler days of the 1800s, and other trails she had blazed herself, creating connections and shortcuts between the older and divergent paths.

Lyra knew her way around like the back of her hand, and she knew how to get most directly to specific wilderness landmarks, forest features, and to special riverside views. Hillocks and knolls, ridges and ravines, brooks and streams—were her waypoints and her guides.

While on foot, she also used universal signs to keep herself oriented. She was blessed with her own internal true north. She was always aware of the height of the sun in the day for any given season, and therefore she could always tell the approximate time of day. Cloudy days were more challenging for time-of-day estimation, and despite this, Lyra was still very comfortable in her awareness of time and place and space.

Lost?

Striding out, Lyra noticed a feather lying on the path, resting on a bed of dry fallen leaves. The feather was long and black, and somewhat tufted looking—like it had been crushed on impact with something.

Her mind flew into overdrive. Why was this feather here, now? Who did it belong to? Did it hurt the bird to lose it? Was there a fight? A violent moment? Maybe old feathers are preened and plucked out at the right time, in the fastidious self-grooming rituals of the bird. Maybe the feather had lost its airfoil function, in being so irregular and tufty, and it just naturally fell out while the bird was in flight. Maybe the bird doesn't even know that it was gone?

Lyra marveled at the exquisite perfection of the feather. Multiple soft and downy projections, parallel layers, tapers, and fluffy sections. Color patterns and markings. Stunning detail and precision and so much function in one single black feather!

She bent down and reached out with her left hand to touch the softness of the plume—to experience the finery of the lone fallen feather.

All of a sudden, she startled. Abruptly she stood up straight. She gasped. Her beautiful Celtic braided gold bangle was missing from her left wrist! Gone! She felt a wave of panic—of sheer dread—at the thought of losing her treasured gift.

Her own nana, Nana-Rose Buchanan, knew Lyra's heart and she knew of Lyra's highly symbolic world. In the 1990s, when Lyra had shared with her nana, her newfound insights about the Celtic braids, Nana-Rose had walked over to her jewelry box and picked something up and brought it back over to Lyra. She said lovingly "Here, Lyra. I want you to have this. Your grandfather gave this braided rose gold bangle to me a very long time ago, and I think you will enjoy having it. You already have an appreciation for the deeper meaning and the symbolism of the braid, like he did. Wear it and be strong in its meaning." Lyra had put the braided bangle on her wrist immediately, and then she hugged her nana. She still wore it almost daily, nearly thirty years later.

And there, in the forest, it was gone! The beautiful braided bracelet was gone! Lyra was mortified. She felt like she was disappointing both of her grandparents in losing the treasured bangle. Her grandfather had died long ago, in the 1970s, and her nana had died at age 101, right at the turn of the century. But despite them being gone for such a long time, she still felt awful about losing the braid. She felt like she had just lost her link, her connection to her grandparents. The strength of their bond was weakened, or so it felt then and there.

A wave of nausea washed over her. Her heart started pumping wildly, and banging hard in her chest. *What am I to do?*

She started walking back on the path, toward the pond, darting her gaze erratically back and forth, to and fro, and all around. She got all the way back to the rock settee by the pond where she had sojourned with Zoli earlier. She knew—she was certain—that she had had the bracelet on her wrist back then. She clearly remembered when she had lifted Zoli up to eye level, with Zoli on her left index finger. She could picture the bracelet on her forearm in that moment. She was sure of it. She distinctly remembered noting to herself at that time how similar the fine braided pattern was to the finely veined matrices of the dragonfly wings. Both, in Lyra's eyes, were delicate and beautiful, yet strong—fine yet formidable. The wonders of the braid!

Lyra repeatedly retraced her steps on that part of the pathway. Six times—back and forth—desperately hoping to find the bangle. She cried.

I bet some animal that is attracted to shiny things has already picked it up and has taken it away somewhere to examine it, to play with it, to covet and cherish it. Or, maybe when it slid off my wrist, it bounced off the beaten path and I'll never find it. And if it bounced into the pond or into the stream, it's surely long gone by now.

Lyra was back at the place where she first found the tufty black feather. She stared at it again, this time with a dullness in her eyes—a lackluster in her demeanor. She felt drained and defeated. But, reality was slowly setting in. *I never, ever give up, but I feel I must. What are the odds of me finding my bracelet here in the woods? What are the chances? I have to move on. Oh, my heart is breaking, with guilt, with shame, and with embarrassment. The bangle could be anywhere now.*

Dear God, I cannot believe this is happening. I should never have been wearing the bracelet out here in the woods, in the first place. What was I thinking? I obviously wasn't thinking at all. It's all my fault. Dear Nana and Grandpops, I'm sorry. So sorry. I was irresponsible, and now the braid is gone. Please forgive me.

In her sadness, she walked on. She knew that in time, she'd get over this. It was a material thing, yes, but for her, it had great sentimental and symbolic significance.

Lyra sighed. She wasn't perfect. Life wasn't perfect. The world wasn't perfect. Perfect didn't exist. She strode on, picking up her spirit a little, with each step. No use being depressed over spilled milk, or lost jewels, or wayward braids. The sun was shining. The day was still young. The path was calling.

Little Things

Up ahead this path led straight into a meadow, rock-strewn with tall grasses waving. A veritable boulder garden! Lots of direct sunlight there, and often a stronger breeze would come through the open space. And for sure, there would be sightings of many creatures. One could witness so many wildlife species in their own lofty-air homes and meadowland playgrounds. It was a delight to be there, in the right place and at the right time.

Lyra trekked onward, knowing that very soon she would come across a large-diameter fallen tree. She could nimbly climb over it and continue on her hike, or, she could choose to sit and linger awhile. Its thick bark was still intact after all this time, and it was softened and weather worn, forming a wee scooped, hollowed seat. It was just the perfect height and size to accommodate her 5'10" lanky form. There were some thick green patches of moss on the damp underside. The tree had been laying on its side for a long time. At the edge of the meadow, there were some unusual hanging mosses, thready and wispy, making the scene ethereal, much like an ancient Irish mystical forest. *Where are those mischievous leprechauns now?*

She walked up to the old fallen tree and sat on it, facing south, with the warm August sun passing almost directly overhead. *Hmmmmm . . . . It must be noon-ish.* Her mind turned to Paidi, for a brief moment. She remembered having Paidi there, out in the meadow, on previous walks. When Paidi ran through the taller grasses, she had to bound with every step to see where she was going. It was a comical sight! Paidi was a calm, easygoing lap dog, and Lyra had always thought that this bounding behavior seemed out of character for her wee Paidi-pie. But, she did need to see where she was going, so, bound she did! Paidi's name was from the Irish Gaelic word paidir, meaning "prayer" or "prayed for." Paidi indeed, was prayed for. An answered prayer. A friend indeed.

Paidi wore a thin grey leather collar at all times. It was embellished with three large oval moonstones. Semiprecious stones for Lyra's superprecious pup. Moonstones are all about inner clarity and inner Light—adularescence and adularia. Lyra was deeply drawn to these words. Moonstones seem to be lit from within. This notion captivated Lyra.

While she was just sitting still in the direct sunlight in the meadow, Lyra took a moment to pull up her hair. She gathered up her long curly tresses, amassing them atop her head, securing them with her ever-present right wrist scrunchie. A few of the tendrils escaped, curling down her long neck. This updo would most definitely keep her cool in the warming day. She mused again, this time out loud "How did I ever get to be so white-haired?" She smiled knowingly. Through her work in the ER and all of her long hours of shift work, she knew exactly how she had earned every single white strand!

Throughout her life, Lyra had been enchanted by the stories of the mystical hair-powers of Samson, Bathsheba, and Rapunzel. Even by Arya of modern day Zortaire Mythology. From her early years, Lyra knew in her heart of hearts, that her then-golden curls—her crowning glory—empowered her in some sort of fanciful, fantastical way. And, as time meandered, the gold became silver, became white—a sparkling and brightest white. Her locks did indeed grow thinner, wispier—fine and unruly with age but they most surely remained a large part of her outward image—open, breezy, flowing and free. Her tresses spoke of her personality, symbolic of her true inner self. There was certainly nothing stuck, or staid, or contrived, about Lyra's curls. Her white sparklescence gave her an aura. A whimsical air. She lived and breathed a purest poesy of persona. No panache. No lofty airs. Approachable. Simply wholesome—fresh and curly, and real.

Lyra was still a little warm. She rolled up the sleeves of her lightweight cardigan—up past her elbows. She smiled as she caught sight of her vibrant full-sleeve tattoos. Her body art showcased images near and dear to her heart, symbols that Lyra herself had designed. Ten years earlier, she had been on a bucket list quest to create some self-defining tattoos. It was a most affirming process, sharing her artful visions with tattoo artists who could see and share in the wonder of her visions. Lyra became a living, breathing, body canvas. Over a period of seven years, one by one, her imaginative images appeared on both of her arms. Her whole back became a watercolor-styled dreamscape. Her true colors were there for all to see.

Raven Life

Lyra called out loud to Creation "What a glorious morning in God's Creation to just hike through these familiar woods and to follow my nose as I please. Hello Mother Nature! You are beautiful! You are just lovely in all your summer finery!" She heard no echoes, nor any answers.

As she sat there, she could hear a noisy ruckus in the distance at the end of the meadow, where tall trees lined the edges of the forest. She tuned in to these sounds to see if she could discern the origin. *For sure these were bird sounds. Were they angry? Upset? Alarmed? Warning their mates?* There was a large nest up high in the trees. She could make out the forms of two large black birds now, flying in repetitive circles over something and occasionally nosediving downward into the meadow. It sounded intense.

Crow versus raven? She had lots of practice over the years, identifying birds by their sounds, their beak shapes, their markings and their size.

"Ravens." she said decisively out loud. "They make distinct grating, grinding and clicking sounds that communicate their precise needs to other ravens. They communicate their messages well."

She thought, *I've seen this flight pattern and these sounds before. I think a larger predator bird must have ventured too close to their nest in the trees, and they are protecting their own young. Those must be a mommy and a daddy raven—lifemates—protecting their nest of either eggs, or chicks or fledglings. I remember reading about how very intelligent and innovative ravens can be, especially when alarmed or protecting their family. If I look closely again at this flight pattern, I bet I'll see—Yup—there it goes—the ravens are flying over the advancing predator and dropping small rocks or stones on the invader bird to either injure it or to scare it off. Look, there's another rock just dropped. I wonder if I'll get to see the predator take off and fly away? There goes another dropped rock. Hey! The tall meadow grasses are rustling madly over there. Ahhhh—oh my—it's a hawk, taking off from the ground—flying away. I hope it doesn't have any chicks in its mouth or in its talons. That would be so sad to see. It's turning this way—closer—almost overhead—Yay! No chicks with the hawk! I'm so relieved! I know this is just nature's way, but I don't need to witness the sad parts. I'm glad the ravens have such good smarts about them, that they could ingeniously protect their young.*

Lyra breathed a heavy sigh of relief. Her mind then methodically cycled backwards through a great long list of raven trivia which was filed in her memory—the comprehensive details that she had amassed through her nature readings, of once upon a time. These details flooded her consciousness.

Ravens richly populate all of the Northern Hemisphere continents, and symbolically this signifies their worldliness and their inherent worldly wisdom. Literally, they are everywhere. They are very intellectual and quick to learn and always discovering new ways to adapt to their environments. And their cognitive abilities and creative thinking have carried them well, as they are in absolutely no danger of extinction, and their numbers are growing.

She remembered too, that the Ancient Celtic folks had a unique proverb "There is wisdom in a raven's head." The Celtic people looked up to the raven for their very high ranking within the animal world. For the ravens are truly seers, they are prophetic. They are sages, and worldly wise. And, they are innovative engineers, quick problem solvers. The ravens, by their intellect and quick thinking, have always been able to stay one step ahead of their predators. They impeccably embody the modern phrase: "Knowledge is power!"

She recalled a bit more raven trivia. *Bird researchers have shown that juvenile unpaired male ravens "hang out" in small flocks, hoping to attract the attention and the favor of nearby unmated females. They put on incredible aerial acrobatic shows, demonstrating their daring, strength, speed and maneuverability—which are all esteemed qualities of a perfect mate! These same juvenile male ravens also show extremely inquisitive behaviors. They notice shiny things, and they are always interested in new, novel, or unusual things. All of these traits point to the ongoing building of the ravens' perceptive vision, street smarts and superior cognitive skills. No wonder they are symbols of wisdom, worldly ways, and think-on-the-fly adaptability!*

Lyra looked up, high in the sky, still facing south. She raised her hand upward, to shield her sage-green eyes from the noonday solar brilliance. It was so breathtakingly bright in the moment, in the Light.

She smiled at what she saw. Far beyond the towering nest in the trees, in the grand celestial heights, she witnessed some of the neighborhood ravens' acrobatics. *I wonder where the female ravens' peanut gallery is? On the ground? In the trees? These guys are really putting on a show!*

Up, up, up higher they'd soar, with their black feathered wings outstretched some more, to catch the maximum airfoil lift. Their silhouettes were dark and stark. Such a powerful contrast against the great blue cathedral dome over the meadow! She could almost make out the individual feather tips! Such architectural beauties those mighty wings were!

The ravens' playfulness almost appeared to be choreographed as they all took turns, performing their kamikaze feats—a sudden beak-first nosedive with a late 'Pull out! Pull out!' leveling off just above the distant trees—or, a balletic, controlled spiral descent, soaring with their wings perfectly set in the vertical plane—or, what appeared to be a synchronized flying duet while soaring in paired circles, to the right and left, drafting seemingly upward. Those female raven onlookers should be mightily impressed by these talented young males.

The meadow was notably silent now. The ruckus was over, and she had seen enough of the air show. Time to relax, to chill. Time to retreat into silence—to find that quiet place again, deep in her soul. *Okay. Time to tune out the trivia and to—just—be. This nature walk and communing time will be over before I even get as far as the deep forest! Enough already!*

Engaging

She closed her eyes and lifted her face upward, into the overhead sun. In this open body posture, she offered her deepest Sacred sound "Ommmmm . . . ." to engage in the ancient rhythm—the soundsong of the universe.

Right there on the log, in the sun, in the middle of nowhere, how could she not do this? It was instinctive. It was proper. She felt called to connect with the earth, with the universe, with the Sacred—she needed to feel that coveted oneness. And she was doing just that.

After minutes of stillness, her inward focus was interrupted. She had noted a fine crackling sound nearby, and there was a new scent in the air. She held her pose and her stillness, and she just let those two notions enter her mind and then exit again.

"Ommmmm . . . ." And after another minute she was distracted again, by the sense of something moving to her left. This time she responded by opening her eyes and looking to the left. She was pleasantly surprised and calm.

A very large raven—a seemingly larger than life-sized raven—had landed on the fallen tree, just beyond her reach. She didn't dare move at all, lest the bird be startled and either attack or retreat. Instead, she just gazed with awe upon this sage queen of the skies.

All of her black body feathers and long tail feathers actually danced and iridesced in shades of royal purple and royal blue in the sunlight.

Lyra could see the brown-grey shaggy feather colorations forming an extraordinary collared necklace, which adorned the raven's slim neck and throat.

Lyra stifled her chuckle. *That's some elegant chic statement piece that she's wearing in the rough and tumble backwoods!* Lyra marveled at the raven's presence and grandeur, for she was a really big bird. Lyra didn't feel alarmed in the least. In her meditative posture, she herself was more still than the raven, who was shifting her weight from right talons to left, quite frequently. *Who knows why the raven is shifting? Anxious? Sore? Restless? Unsure?*

Lyra inwardly chided herself. *Lyra, Stop assessing the bird like it was one of your patients! Just stop getting yourself bogged down with the infinitesimal details! It doesn't matter why! Just enjoy your precious moment with the wisest of all ancient birds and animals!*

Communing

The raven hailed out to Lyra, cocking its head to the left. "Hello Lyra, my name is Yala! I am a Celtic mystical raven, and I have lived at the edge of this meadow for many years now with my mate. Once again we have some of our own young fledglings that are about to leave the nest.

"I've seen you walking in and around this area for years and I know where you live, over by the mouth of the River Saye. I can tell that you feel at home here. You are just so comfortable in the meadow. I hope I'm not disturbing you."

Lyra smiled. *This is an exquisite moment. I am so fully tuned in to my natural world that I am actually hearing a meadowland raven who, throughout her spacious life, has literally soared through life in the skies, seeing the world from a prodigious worldly perspective. And she is speaking to me!*

Lyra quietly answered, "No, Yala, you're not disturbing me at all. I want for us to connect and learn from each other and share in each others' worlds. Can we do that here? Can we do that now?"

Lyra gazed into Yala's dark brown eyes. Hers was a soft inquisitive look, and Yala returned the gesture with her own most encouraging facial expression, for indeed she was the wisest elder of all living species.

OPEN YOUR MIND

"Lyra, I have something important to tell you. You have a lot of growing, self-awareness building and identity seeking to do. I am the raven. I live and play in the wide-open skies. I am the symbol all around the world of intelligence, worldly wisdom, and adaptability. And before I teach you any-thing more about the high priority and importance of all of these, I must teach you this.

"You must open your mind to worldly wisdom! There is so much sub-lunary knowledge out there at your fingertips, but unless you open your mind to *all* of the worldly-wisdom resources, then even the most basic knowledge is of little or no value to you. For an obvious example, it would be like you approaching a magical mystical well, brimming with waters that have all the healing and transformative powers that you desire. It's all use-less to you unless you bring a cup or a straw or a bucket or a spoon, and then open your mouth! The resource is there but you have to intentionally open yourself to it.

"The whole wide world is full of sages and seers, researchers and scholars, and they are all there at your fingertips. Once you open your mind to the vastness of knowledge, to the grace of knowledge, you will for sure be on an ideal path. You cannot grow and "become" if you choose to stay be-hind locked doors in your tiny limited life. You need a worldly-knowledge base and a worldly perspective. You need to be out in the wide world, sens-ing, listening, learning, immersing, and challenging, with everything that is new and unexplained.

"When you open your mind, your worldly vision and your worldly wisdom increases. So does your understanding and your ability to stand up and have an opinion. Then you can use your voice to advocate for impor-tant issues and concerns. Your ever-curious, truth-seeking desire and your spirit of inquiry also increase with your worldly exposures.

"Is this too big or too small for you? Can you feel the greatness of my wish? Will you choose to move forward on your journeys, intentionally opening your mind to worldly wisdom, in all your life circumstances?"

Lyra's eyes were wide open. She was awestruck, trying to tune in to an unmistakable aura surrounding her. She was encircled by a phenomenal presence, and her mind had the uncanny feeling of lightness, of stretch-ing outward, of pushing out the perimeters of her boney cranial vault. She remembered to breathe. In so doing, all of the pressures and the lightness, and the stretching sensations—all of these perceptibly increased again.

When she took her next breath, her own doubts and fears took over and she cried out

"I don't know how to do this! I am trying! But, the top of my head is going to blow off! This is beyond anything I've ever known and this is unnerving me!"

Yala responded "Lyra, my dear one, opening your mind is not a literal bodily thing. Rather, it is conceptual and experiential—but not in a physical sense. It is an invitation to you to un-clutter your consciousness. Opening your mind involves the ability to tap into the influential voices of the mystical grounds of your own spirituality, like you're doing right now! Choose to tap into worldly scholarly voices. Tap into the powerful learned voices in your own faith tradition. You are indeed wonderfully made. You are colorfully, contemplatively, and spiritually made!"

Yala spoke softly, with her ever-encouraging tone. "Lyra, look up to the sky and see. See the universal sky. It is the same limitless dome that encircles the whole earth. And way up there in the universe, are the stars and the planets and the galaxies and all elements of the cosmos. That sky is incomprehensibly vast and mostly unknown. And, mostly not yet understood. To the open mind, there are no limits, no boundaries, no conditions on the power of knowledge. To the open mind, there is space and room for the all the wonders of worldly wisdom. To the open mind, there is all the potential in the world, for full discovery and discernment of the subtleties and the complexities of all worldly truths."

Lyra, had been looking up, gazing, as Yala had requested. But, in her complete awe and wonderment, she was almost in tears. "This is so overwhelming. I am so small. I am well educated, yes. But really, I'm not all that worldly. And Yala, you're asking such great things of me. How can I possibly comprehend this, and embody this all-encompassing worldly vision and open-mindedness in my everyday life?" She stopped speaking, lest her words be wasted and her emotions take over her inborn powers of critical thinking.

She also remembered that God had asked some very great things of some of the most unexpected people of biblical times. Monumental things, of truly ordinary folks like Moses, Elijah, David, and Mary and Joseph. In her present state of overwhelm, Lyra's tears were flowing freely.

Yala watched her closely. She simply allowed time itself to move on, and for Lyra's river of tears to flow their natural course. Lyra and Yala both became silent. Theirs was a sweet silence, connecting their souls. It was almost like a soothing, healing balm was settling around Lyra. Her head felt normal again. That outward stretching sensation completely subsided.

Lyra could once again breathe easily and relax all her muscles. She slowly twisted her torso even more to the left, to face Yala squarely. In the moment, Yala was perfectly still, poised and balanced on all talons, on the ancient tree bark pulpit.

Gratitude

"Thank you Yala, for the gift of your presence and for the blessing of your wisdom. I treasure everything you've told me, and I will continue and ponder these things in my heart. You've given me so much to think about and to work with. I feel encouraged by your wisdom and by your very presence. I know I'll never ever forget this meadowland encounter with you under the high and wide indigo sky."

Lyra added "And since you Yala, and all ravens, are deemed to be worldly—you are sages, seers and engineers—I'll name my personal takeaway from the ravens. I affirm that I will carry with me the desire to grow in worldly wisdom, always. Not simply in knowing just enough to merely to get by or to survive. Rather, to open my mind to worldly wisdom like you Yala, like all of the ravens, in order to thrive, in order to fly high and be wise, to see and to know the broader, wider world. Oh, to see from the skies! Seize the knowledge—Seize the day—Seize my new identity and my place in this world!

"In all seriousness though, between Zoli and yourself, I will live out my days with open eyes and an open mind, knowing of the spiritual and mystical wonders that this openness can bring to my life."

Lyra continued "Yala, My heart is full of gratitude for you and your message. I simply chose to go for a walk in the woods, humble in heart, simply wishing to clear my head. And, without my even asking, I have been approached mystically, spiritually, and relationally. The voices I've heard are full of relevant teachings, with insights into my own life. They are going to be so helpful for my future.

"It's like I've tuned into a special auditory channel, or playlist, or even a wavelength that is being broadcasted just for me in this moment. I am the tangible receiver for these most intangible lessons and encouraging words. And Yala, I am humbled, in being approached with these profound messages. I am humbled to simply be in the presence of such beneficent messengers. I am humbled to be called to receive these exquisite words and wisdom. My heart bows in deep gratitude. My mind gratefully responds by opening comprehensively. My thankful soul awakens to the mystery and to the wonder of the depth of the moment!"

Yala graciously blessed Lyra, uttering softly in a kind and loving warbling sound as she lifted off, homeward bound, into the curve of the wide, open skies.

The Word of God
In Real Time—In Prayer

My Beloved,
Allow yourself to be transformed
by the renewing of your mind,
that you may discern my will,
that which is good
and acceptable and perfect.
Blessed be your mindful transformation, My Beloved. Amen.

Into the Deepest Well

Meet Bradn—the Celtic Salmon

Within me rests the deepest of wells—a wellspring crude and vast—
Where echoes of Eternal Sounds—rise up from eons past.
Profound the Celtic sagacious Voice—so resonant and real—
Whose ripples surge as Sacred Truths—fresh mystical appeal.

Beauty in Nature

The meadow was strangely silent. The noontime breeze had subsided completely, leaving an eerie hush, almost like a vacuum of emptiness was hanging there in the wilderness. Lyra tuned in to the quiet. *Is this real, or is this emptiness of sound simply a fallout sensation of my recent cranial overload and my spiritual sensory overstimulation? Is this silence a sweet and sensory gift to me from God, given in the name of leading me more fully into an inner realm of peace? Is this possibly the proverbial calm before the storm, even though I know what the fair-weather forecast said? Hmmmmm . . . .*

Lyra could not possibly have known just there and then, the predictive powers of her words. She was in for one emotional rollercoaster ride, and a mixed bag of highs and lows. She was about to experience both a sprinkling and a showering of widely contrasting emotions—wonder, compassion, self-doubt, darkening angst, and gratitude. And, a curious impartment of knowledge, mystery and mystique awaited her. Her "storm senses" were indeed poised, piqued. They were almost prophetic. No matter what was to come, Lyra was open, receptive, ready.

Still perched on the fallen tree, she turned her attention to the ground beneath her. In the mostly dry earth, she could see multiple imprints of little birds' feet, facing in every which direction. Tiny and perfect little V-shapes in the dirt.

Sometimes, she liked to work through things out loud. "The meadow is yet another microcosm, and all life here is interconnected unto itself. There are layers of dependent, independent, and interdependent behaviors here, even symbiotic too. Some of these I will witness over time, and others will remain a mystery to me. For sure!"

Just a little over to her left, in the meadowland grass, something caught her eye. It was not moving, but its texture was unique. She bent low, to study it. With her face close to the ground, she cast no shadow from the overhead sun. She could see clearly there and then, in the Light.

"Wow!" she uttered slowly. Cast off where it lay, was a long, slim, opaque snakeskin shed. It was in one complete piece. Delicate, ghostlike and mysterious, it pointed yet again to the wonders of all Creation.

Lyra had no intention of touching it, but she took a few moments to remain with the shed and to pore over its intricate form. It had an ivory-grey-mauve-taupe coloring that stood stark in contrast to the vitality of its backdrop of meadowland green blades rising. It was fragile and feather-weight. Despite its fascinating beauty, it had already served its sole purpose in life. It lay there, abandoned by its original owner. Symmetrical rings encircled the circumference, and these band patterns were uninterrupted for the whole length of the shed. She noted some smaller, finer segments on the sides of the shed, that were detailed with a honeycomb, or a geometric pattern of interlocking octagons. Such innate and perfectly repeating patterns! Her eyes were wide with delight.

Lyra recalled learning about some mathematical applications in high school. Her math teacher had said something like, "Patterns in nature are simply visible regularities of physical form found in the natural world. These perfect patterns recur and repeat in many different contexts in nature. Repeating patterns in nature and order in nature are simply, pure math!"

Fractals and spirals—snakeskins and snailshells—are pure geometry.
A simple pinecone and an intricate snowflake both mimic Sacred geometry!
The angles of the branches of the Tree of Life can be measured! They are all
predictable and calculable. They all compel an onlooker's intrigue, merely by
their perfection. I've never forgotten this famous "image of nature" analogy,
in of all places, my math class! It makes complex mathematical applications
come alive! It makes math relevant and applicable. It makes math real! Thank
you, math-life master, Mr Claire! She smiled.

Patterns, and Truth of Life

Lyra's mind wandered to another special mentor, Kirk Wipper. He was a
Canadian outdoor education guru, who loved to share his wisdom and
his earthy philosophies with his young adult students. He literally opened
their eyes to mindfulness in the natural world. He sharpened their senses
in attuning to their surroundings. On any given nature hike Kirk would
frequently stop, and be still. He'd simply call out the word "patterns", while
pointing to sands on the shores, fungi in forests, tree bark and leaves, and
sounds of the breeze. His students would also stop, notice, and focus. Kirk's
word "patterns" became a cue word—a signal. It became a formative lens
through which his students could witness and perceive and appreciate all
of Creation's wonders. His wife, Ann, would say "Kirk's inborn sense of
wonder was, simply contagious!"

Lyra reflected fondly and recalled yet another memorable moment, an
aha moment with Kirk. One evening a long time ago around the campfire,
Kirk had extrapolated the words of English poet William Wordsworth. He
said "Let Nature be your teacher. She will show you the ultimate truth of
life. Living in respect and acceptance of nature are essential tools for living
and for survival."

Lyra delighted in all of Kirk's approaches. She was acutely aware that
her own inquisitive lust for nature, and her deeper understanding of the
cycles of life, all stemmed from her learning from this mountain of a man.
It warmed her heart to call him friend.

She glanced once more at the snakeskin shed and then she straightened up and stretched. It was time to move along.

Lyra stood up, careful not to sliver herself on the old bark. *No need for*
injuries out here in the wilds. No seasoned, safety conscious emergency nurse

worth her salt is going to face or endure any harm—or hardship—secondary to her own carelessness or recklessness! Not me anyway!

She moved through the patches of tall grasses by the log. They tickled on her long, well-muscled legs. When she returned to the trail, she set a good pace, moving toward the edge of the clearing and into the gnarly deciduous forest once again.

Once into the cooling shade of the forest, she felt a welcomed relief from the warmth of the overhead sun. The high ceiling of broad green leaves created a dappled light "pattern" on the ground. They blocked some of the sun from reaching her on the path. Unique. Beautiful. They were one-of-a-kind patterns, moments of Light. She smiled fondly and said boisterously, out loud "Thank you, Kirk!"

Random Act of Compassion

Up ahead, the path arose in a short, steeply inclined slope only to continue on, on the flats, for a long stretch. Lyra could see something at the top of the incline, but couldn't make out its form. As she got closer, she realized that the small soft furry beige creature was laying on its side, not moving.

"A bunny!" she whispered. Its lifeless form lay in stillness on its side. Not even enough breeze to rustle the silky fur. Lyra got up to the top of the slope and immediately squatted down beside the beautiful animal. Its large brown eye was still open, staring, as if transfixed in its gaze. She touched the fur, noting that it wasn't even cool to touch yet, indicating that the death was very recent indeed.

Likely it was chased by a fast or nimble predator. Perhaps a fox. There are no obvious signs of blood or trauma, so the bunny likely died instantly after being shaken violently, breaking its neck.

Why was the bunny unceremoniously left where it was, in plain sight, on the trail? If it had been killed by another animal, perhaps the predator had been suddenly startled away? Maybe, I myself startled the fox? Maybe it had to abruptly leave the coveted prize of precious wee bunny behind? The poor predator had masterfully conquered the kill, but didn't get to savor the succulent feast for supper. Poor ol' fox!

Lyra's compassionate heart stepped up into high gear. "I cannot just leave this animal here. Some large bird of prey, or a carnivore is going to come along and totally disrespect this little body. I must protect it. I must bury it so that at least the bunny's body has some dignity in death." She wondered what she could use for digging.

A sturdy-looking fallen branch nearby, that had a splintered edge, would do the trick. She got busy with her makeshift stick-shovel and started to dig a shallow grave just off the north side of the trail. Digging with her rustic implement was relatively effortless, as the soil broke up easily with the dampness and the moisture of the recent rains still lingering in the earthen depths.

A few minutes later, she accomplished her task and she gingerly placed her hands under the limp furry form and lowered it into the earthen grave. Thoughtfully, tenderly, she pulled up a few blades of grass, and a lift of moss, and placed these in front of the little bunny's nose, in the grave. Then, the hard part came where she had to scoop the loamy earth back over top of the bunny. She reminded herself, *Better this way than at the mercy of the carnivores.*

A small white butterfly fluttered by, and seemed to hover, watching her work, while she remained squatted at the crude woodland graveside. With the grave now completely closed over and patted down, she took time to cover it with forest debris. She stood back, rubbing the dirt out of her hands. Seeking out a befitting grave marker, she chose a nearby hefty rock and nestled it like a headstone over the newly-turned earth.

"There. That's it. Done." She felt emotional, but she was not in tears. She knew about the inherent dangers that herbivores faced every single day in the forest, as the larger carnivores were always on the hunt. She knew that she couldn't help *all* herbivores, but for this little one, her efforts had made a dignified difference at its end of life. This warmed her heart.

With her hands held together prayerfully, she stood in quiet reverence beside the grave, and asked God to hold bonnie wee bunny in eternal peace—and in love. She whispered, "Blessed be, bonny bunny, blessed be". Lyra drew in one long breath, allowing her shoulders to raise up high on inspiration, and then allowing herself to fully relax, her shoulders sinking downward in her full emptying expiration. And she moved on.

As she walked along, she thought about the cycles of life in the forest, putting everything in perspective. She feared that the smallest creatures must truly feel helpless and even powerless against the bigger predators. But, hunting means food and survival. Predators hunt to survive. Tiny bunny was just a little link in the chain of life, in the food supply, in the circle of life. Lyra stuck to her guns though, and she felt good in having protected the bunny's dignity in death. Lyra's heart was big enough for all the hurting, and the sorrowing, and the grieving, even in the food chain of the wider animal world.

Hard Questions

Lyra continued to muse. *What if I had never become a nurse? What kind of heart would I have? Was I born with compassion, as in Nature theory? Would I still have been as compassionate, wanting to help and make a difference to people, to animals, to the world? Or did nursing actually fine-tune my compassionate heart? Did my compassionate heart only open up to blossom when I became a nurse, as in Nurture theory?*

I often think about the hungry, but I don't choose to work in the food bank. I often worry about the mental health outpatients who are alone at Christmas, but I don't volunteer my time at the drop-in mental health center in town. My church has outreach programs that I financially contribute to, but am I really making any difference in this way? Is my compassion truly, all-encompassing and unconditional, or is it sadly, shamefully, selective? I seem to be favoring wee bunnies over cunning foxes! Could I perhaps be doing better in the Social Justice realm? Hmmmmm . . . .

She recalled, a Scripture in Micah, which had been formative for her throughout her nursing career. God asks us "to do justice, love kindness, and to walk humbly with (our) God." And then, Philippians 2, reminded her that *all* people could choose to "be of the same mindset of Christ." They *all* could choose to embody the phrase "Christlike Living" in their own daily lives. Lyra had enjoyed learning about the mission work, in the travels of Saint Paul, "The Odyssey of Saint Paul," as coined by contemporary theologians. She liked the term, Pauline Christianity and its nickname, "Gentle Christianity." In the beautiful forest realm, Lyra expanded on these thoughts out loud. In her oversimplifying way, she calculated:

Christ = Love. Love = Compassion. Compassionate Living = Christlike Living.

Lighthearted, she concluded out loud "I *can* do this! I *am* doing this! I *do* live my life in Christlike Living. She resolved, "But—I could still do more. I could choose to do more." In slang verbing she whispered "I could human better."

Out of the blue, those two powerful Scriptures and many other questions, bombarded her brain. They swept through her mind, like a rogue ocean wave. She asked herself some very direct questions, which raised doubts about the authenticity of her compassionate heart.

Well, the relentless storming by all of these questions was just too overwhelming and she faltered. She failed to answer them, in that moment. *Truth—down to earth soul-searching naked-reality truth—is hard to face. I am so conflicted! Maybe I'm not truly the compassionate soul that I feel I am, or I'm not all that I could be. Maybe I'm not, everything I think I am, and my compassionate heart really doesn't measure up. Perhaps I just don't want to face the honest truth about the possible shallowness and selfishness of my own naked heart and my core conditional compassion?*

I don't feel guilty or judged for any of this. Rather, the sagging weights of ineptitude and inadequacy are pressing inward on my heart. I feel rattled, and confused. What is truth? How deep do I have to go, to find the real buried truth? Hmmmmm . . . .

She cried out loud "Truthfully, honestly, Who am I? What am I? I don't even know my own heart! I am all over the place. Compassionate? Yes! No! Sometimes? Selectively? Dear God, this conflict—these unanswered questions—are tearing at my heart." Her tears began to flow. Full on streams of salty tears flooded down her tanned cheeks. She felt a growing lump in her throat.

"It's okay to cry," she said out loud to herself. "I am human. I am a human yoyo. My emotions fluctuate. But that's because I care, so deeply. Life truly is a roller coaster on any given day. I just need to stay with my feelings. I need to honor them. I need to work things through. I need to let my emotions out, instead of bottling them up inside. No one can see me here in the forest, and I'm just going to let all of these tears fall until there's no more to fall—till my tear-well is all dried up."

And sure enough, in time, the lump in her throat disappeared. Her lips stopped quivering. And the tears did stop. There was no more crying to do, in the moment. Lyra was over it, for the time.

She had continued walking during her tears and chuckled then, about having to go all the way to the depths of the forest just to have a really good cry! She really did see the lighter side of things, often.

Seeing the Light

Her mind meandered, to the story of a middle-aged man she knew through her church. Life as George knew it, was downright tough. His was an abusive father. As a teenager, George was placed into foster care. He was abused there too, and he ran away to live on the streets. He was soon jailed for a year, for theft. He straightened out after getting out and worked for many years earning a laborer's wage. Never married, he was lonely. He felt abandoned and unloved.

In his forties after openly admitting he was suicidal and had a plan to end his life, he received immediate care and counsel through the hospital, and was entered into a most life-changing mental health day program. Afterward he repeatedly expressed his gratitude to Lyra, to his church, and to his community, for believing in him and for assisting him in his darkest hour.

George stopped living in the past—he stopped dwelling on the past. He started valuing himself—valuing his darkness and his Light. He began believing in himself! He smiled more, laughed more, and told funny stories. He made a point of giving back, at church and community events. His heart was full of gratitude. George, in Lyra's mind, became a living synonym for gratitude! George's life was clearly becoming a life of gratitude.

Oh, my goodness! It's time for me to put things back in perspective in my own life! Lyra was suddenly radiant with an epiphanic glow. *I don't need to walk around with a dark cloud around me, or, with a fire in my head, all because I cannot figure out who I am or where I'm going! I'm not living in darkness, murky waters maybe, but not darkness for sure!*

I need to learn a really big life-lesson from George. I need to see the Light. I need to look for the Light everywhere. I need to value myself and my life and my life experiences—all of them! I need to look for the goodness that is all around me, everyday. I need to lighten up, lighten my step, and count my blessings—daily. I need to live in gratitude. I need to acknowledge my gratitude, like George does, every single day. I need to make my heart, a heart of gratitude. Thank you, George! Hmmmmm . . . .

Kissed by the Mist

Lyra had continued walking in the woods as she contemplated gratitude. She could see very clearly, as all of her tears were long gone from her eyes. She came upon a single long-stem wild aster flower. *A Talisman of Love! A stunning blue hue in the green forest scene. The great blue bloom stands up tall and lean. How unusual for it to be flourishing here, in the middle of the forest! For sure, there is ample light for growth, but where on earth did the seed come from? How did it get here? Had a bird picked up a seed in my wildflower garden and flown with it all this way, only to drop it on the forest floor? Or, perhaps a squirrel, or a little chipmunk had transported the seed?*

In anticipation, she gently bent over to sniff, knowing full well that asters have no scent at all. Oh well. She had explored the beauty with her nose, just in case. Her heart had hoped for a sweet gift of floral fragrance, but it was not meant to be. Not every flower could possibly have it all—perfection, beauty, tall willowy stature, fragrance, and deep symbolism. Humans were like that too—not a single soul could possibly have it all. And that was truth. That was life. Time to move on.

Lyra looked up to the blue blue sky, up and away from the blue blue aster. *Pretty, pretty, these two bluest of blues!*

A maple leaf aloft caught her attention momentarily. Its mother tree had just let it go, and Lyra witnessed the lackadaisical earthbound drift. It seemed suspended. Personified, it was not wishing to rush to the ground, not needing to hurry along, just needing to be. It was on a once in a life-time journey of its own, with time to spare and sights to see, everywhere. It swirled—strutting and sashaying—in the moment, in the now. *Oh, dance on the breeze, fanciful, free—your grace and your whimsy are certain to please!*

Lyra immediately identified with the leaf. She saw the symbolic parallel to her present, to her now, to her very being. She voiced out loud "And you lovely leaf, are just like me. *Flaneuses de la forêt* are we. Poetry in a leaf. Poetry in life. Poetry in me. Thanks be!" She sighed in deepest contentment, in wonderment, in bliss. "Hmmmmm . . . ."

The elevation was changing, and Lyra knew that with this slight down-hill descent, that she would soon be coming across a lovely sight to behold. There was a high rocky cliff just ahead, over which fell the fresh waters of a stream en route to its final destination, the River Saye.

Her anticipation grew at the thought of the thirty-foot high cascade of sparkling waters. There was a little path just east of there, which safely led hikers and neighbors down the steep cliff face and over to the base of the waterfall.

Lyra took this route. When she arrived at the base of the falls, she paused and took in a long slow breath. A moisture-laden breath. A lung full of pure, healing, humid air. With sheer delight, she was able to stand on a large rock just near enough to the water to allow the cool, dewy spray to kiss her hair, her face and her body.

What a refreshing delight! How free she felt to just step into the mist, be graced by the mist, be one with mist, if only for a minute or two.

Lyra had fondly nicknamed this waterfall the Irie Falls of the North, for she could see nuances of tiny, dancing "iri-descent" rainbows intermittently appearing in the fine fair mist. They hovered in diffracted pastel color bands.

She reached out her hands and held them under the pounding waterfall. She gave them a really good rub, remembering her toils in her recent burial efforts. She cupped her newly scrubbed hands and brought the clean water up to splash onto her face, and she felt the wonder and the welcome in the coolness on her skin.

She could linger long there, in the moment. She could choose to stay there all day. Her heart was so open to the beauty and the wonder and to the renewing powers of the waters.

As a youngster, Lyra would sometimes hike with her dad for some relaxing afternoon fun back in the woods to the Irie Falls. Sometimes they'd cast a line from the shallows. Sometimes they'd go in under the falls and horse around. Sometimes they'd just sit and talk on the rocky shore with the pure clear waters thundering in their midst.

Her dad was always very busy with his work and with his perpetual projects around the home. He never sat still. As a teenager, he helped out on the farm, but he enlisted with the RCAF during World War II and went on into the world of business after the war. He always worked so hard.

Back then, Lyra cherished her one-on-one time with her dad, there at the falls. He'd tell her stories of his childhood, of when he fished on the shores of the River Saye and then came straggling home late, well after dark with his catch.

He'd tell of the mean and mischievous pranks he played, especially on his younger brother. He had a real hearty laugh, a belly-jiggling laugh. His was a twinkling, green-eyed grin.

He'd also take time at the falls, to ask Lyra what was on her heart—her hopes, her plans, her dreams. They were both very much alike in their ways. Detailed. Methodical. Preplanned and prepared.

They had a simpatico father-daughter relationship. They could see each other's strengths, and they held each other up in mutual respect. Like the magnificent waterfall, her dad was a tower of strength—intrepid and true. She sighed. Memory lane was a lovely place to be.

Lyra sat down on a dry, rounded boulder. She closed her eyes. In her mind's eye, she saw the subtle iridescence. She felt the dance of color and the kiss of the mist. Waters over the falls were like a showering of God's grace to the world. She felt arising in her, gentle waves of appreciation—as she received the gracious gift—the coveted treasure—the priceless gift of God's grace bestowed upon her. She felt uplifted. Valued. Worthy. Affirmed. And most of all, she felt connected. Connected to her ever-present God, through the tangible outpouring of his grace, in the simple vision of coming to stillness beside the great deep-woods waterfall.

Lyra spoke out loud "God is good. God's grace is abundant. God's grace knows no boundaries and is here for all those who open their hearts to receive. God is here with me—thanks be to God."

Lyra sat there in stillness, in wonder, in Creation's splendor, for a good ten minutes. The thunderous sounds of the waterfall entranced her. They formed the ultimate backdrop in perfect juxtaposition, for the stillness of her soul. Delicate dewdrops were forming on the fine hairs of her forearms. Her face felt tickled in the moisture of the mist. Her spirit was floating somewhere aloft, drifting with abandon for a few precious moments. She pondered *Have I been changed? Enlightened? Am I Transcending? Hmm-mmm . . . .* She simply left those compelling questions to play alone by themselves in the mist, as they would.

With all of the fresh living waters moving in her midst—the mist, the falls, the fervent stream—Lyra couldn't help but feel thirsty. She dearly wished she had brought her water bottle, but she hadn't. Then, she longed for her afternoon cup of tea. *Sigh.* While seated on the streamside rock, she felt a strong urge to just reach out to her ever-hot tea pot, to pour herself a cup o' cardamom. She just let that notion go. *I'm on a rock in the woods, not on my rocker, at home!*

Suddenly, something whizzed through her visual field, interrupting her train of thought. She saw where it landed in the fast-flowing, rocky stream, but she couldn't make out its form. She had on other occasions, witnessed small fish hurtling over the ledge at the heights of the falls, only to land in the water and continue their journey downstream, on their journey of life. *Hey! Perhaps what I just saw was an airborne fish, openly playing in the heights, dancing out of the depths, living its best life in the moment, just as I myself am doing?! Just being—believing—beholding—becoming—boldly going—being still—being One! Hmmmmm . . . .*

Lyra came back into real time and felt a wee pang of guilt. As beautiful as the falls were, she knew she must move on. *Maybe it is two-thirty or so? The day is still young!*

It was time to follow the stream, downstream for a piece. This would then loop her deeper into the coniferous forest and connect her with another path that would lead her back home. Lyra knew this shortcut along the stream very well. After her long trek in the warm August heat, that waterfall moment was truly a gift. She felt alive. Engaged. Content. Ready.

Deep, Deeper, and Deepest Celtic Truths

In following the stream, just a few hundred feet away, Lyra knew to look for an ancient spring-fed well. She had been told it was fathoms-deep, although she knew not how true this was. She didn't know of a single soul living in the Buchanan Lakes District who could verify the depth. There were many such deep natural wells in the Lake District. All were just part of the beauty of the ultra-rugged wilderness.

She pondered on the use of the word, *ancient,* for a moment. *Why does everyone say the well is ancient? The forest is truly ancient. The rocks are ancient. The rivers and lakes are ancient, so why do the locals specify that the well is ancient? Perhaps it is just their way of adding mystery and intrigue to the story of their natural world? Perhaps to them, ancient means something uniquely special, or mystical, about the well? Perhaps they say ancient, just because their own grandfathers had said it was?*

She pondered on the word, *deep,* and recalled looking up the word in the dictionary once upon a time. She had been pleased to read of two very accurate and useful definitions. The first was literal, where the word *deep* described a distance, extending far downward from a surface.

The second definition she felt truly and deeply drawn to. It inferred an inherent extremeness or intensity, or a profound nature of something, even a weightiness or heaviness, or richness could be inferred. Lyra truly loved the wonders of words. Words themselves, were deep. She sighed and smiled.

The word was calling her into yet another contemplative query. She recalled learning a lot over the years, about the Celtic Wisdom and the Celtic Christian Tradition.

The ancient Celtic folks worshipped out of doors so that they could be as close to their divine God as possible. They described certain locations, like rugged rocky shorelines, and high windy elevations, as being Thin Places. Places where the separation of the human from the Divine was so very fine and thin.

Thin Places were also likened to a luminous translucent space intimately shared by the human and the Divine. The towering and toppled remains of many grand stone-sculpted freestanding Celtic crosses still exist today in some historically Thin Places. They are found dotting all of the shorelines and rocky precipices throughout the UK. They are a stunning reminder to all today of the timelessness and the enduring power of the mystical Celtic Wisdom and faith tradition.

The Celtic folks loved the words of Saint John in the New Testament, where John The Mystic spoke about the "beginnings." He taught that we, all people, are indeed born *of God*, not merely made *by God*. John also spoke of the Light of God deep within us all. He spoke of God as Light. So too then, we are Light. *The life of the Word is the Light of all people. Life is Light. That's so deep!*

Then, the Celts described the depths within our very being, where a River flows through all time, connecting us to our ancestral and elemental past and to our God and to our faith from all of the ages past. Eternity becomes fluid and flowing, forward and dynamic, in the timelessness of the River deep within.

Beyond the River, deeper still within us is the Light of God. God is the Light Beyond the River. We are one with God. God is Light within us. God is in each of us. We are Sacred. And this is true for all things that live on this earth. The trees are made *of God*, so they are Sacred. The ocean waters are made *of God* and therefore they are Holy.

This is truly, the Celtic way of seeing all life as Holy. They indeed looked for, and they saw, the Holiness in all life forms. And, extrapolating this into their daily lives, they treated all persons and all living things with utmost respect, with compassion and love, and with deep reverence. All life was Sacred, as all were born of God.

The Celtic way of seeing the Sacred in all life had captivated Lyra's big compassionate heart. For some time, she had intentionally embodied this truth in all of her daily living. It was easy for her to do, for she wanted to believe with her whole heart that her own wholesome compassionate ways were, through Celtic eyes, inborn.

Walloped!

Lyra was actually much closer to the well than she thought when she heard a very loud splash. Kerploosha! She turned her head to locate the sound, in time to see large perfect circles of ripples emanating from the center of the well. The well itself was oblong in shape, fifteen feet by twenty-five feet or so, with a rocky ledge on the south side and three other muddy and grassy edges.

She wondered what could have caused the sound and the splash and the amazing ripple effects. Her mind turned briefly to Paidi. Lyra no longer brought Paidi to the well. Something about it upset Paidi, and she would bark incessantly at the deep, dark waters. She sensed something unusual about the well. There was something bigger, or greater than herself, to get excited about. Perhaps she barked in fear. Perhaps she barked in awe. Nonetheless, the barking was an annoyance, a distraction, so Paidi didn't get to come to the well anymore!

Lyra walked up to the edge to get a better look. She saw something glimmering, just under the surface by the edge. It was a large colorfully scaled fish, resplendently attired in its silver, coral and gold bedazzled tunic. "That's strange." she said out loud "As far as I know, no fish dwell in the wells. This is really odd."

The big shimmering fish had glided gracefully through the still waters over to Lyra, and playfully laid over onto its left side. It mischievously flicked a wallop of water into the air, totally drenching Lyra!

She let loose in loud laughter and sheer delight, in the exuberance of the moment with her newfound well-dwelling fish. The soaking well waters made a most welcoming cool sensation course throughout her whole body, bringing excitement to her warm flesh and enlivenment deep down in to her soul. Her spiritual senses became piqued, heightened—and ready.

OPEN YOUR HEART

"Hello Lyra! My name is Bradn! I am a Celtic mystical being. I am a salmon, and I make my home in the deepest wells of life."

"Oh my, hello Bradn! Thanks for the soaking! Whohoo! That felt great! Refreshing!"

Lyra went on "This is just so fascinating, talking to you here by the ancient well. It's almost fantastical! But I am intrigued. Might you have a wonderful life-lesson for me? I'm all ears!"

Bradn was grinning gill to gill. His scales glinted like shimmering sequins and gems. The scales poetically sparkled and flirted with each other in the water and in the light as if they were courting each other. As if they were dancing, romancing, in the luminous watery-well-ballroom.

Bradn continued, "I am so happy that our paths have crossed! You are on such an amazing spiritual journey today, full of magical, mystical, and even barely believable moments and encounters. You are being reminded of Jesus' parable and commanding word *Ephphatha*, meaning "Be opened!" You are learning about being open, fully open, in order to truly appreciate the wonders of life all around you—all in order to maximize your experiential identity quest—all in order to ultimately lead you to becoming most fully human.

"Your personal formation and transformation journeys are carrying you well on your way. You have learned to open your eyes to the possibilities of becoming more fully human and to open your mind to the realm of worldly wisdom. Are you ready now to turn inward, profoundly inward, to open your heart? To open your heart to the well of inner wisdom that lies deep within your very heart and soul?"

Lyra was excited. So excited that she spoke out in a flight of ideas, with accelerated speech and elevated voice tones. Bradn astutely noted her heightened state. Lyra rambled on "Yes, of course, I'd love to talk about open hearts, and depth of the heart, and anything you'd like to tell me about my heart. I'm so ready. So primed!" She stopped to catch her breath.

She paused to recall some very wise words shared with her by her church friend, Peter. Being a man of few words, he had once told Lyra about his mom's sage advice. Peter's mom had tenderly asked him during his formative years to choose to speak with reserve. Always. To hold back. To speak only when words would complement the message. To speak only when and if words would be helpful or meaningful. Silence was okay. Silence was healthy. Silence was sometimes better than words. And deliberate economy of words often packed way more clout than verbosity in overdrive. Peter's mom's words rang out so true, there, by the well. Lyra realized, in the moment, the excessiveness, and wastefulness, of her current bumbling, tumbling words. She was most surely, not speaking with reserve.

Before she could babble on any further, Bradn intentionally cut her off, by blowing a long string of big noisy bubbles at her. Lyra got the subtle message and settled right down. She was ready to listen and learn.

Bradn spoke slowly, in his calm, bass-level tones "I want to open your heart. I want to take you deeper in your own understanding of the depths within. I know that you are a compassionate woman. I can see this in your whole person. I see it in the way you've cared for all of your emergency and parish patients, and neighbors, and family—and strangers alike—even the little forest animals and flowers. You respect them—you treat them all with respect. You tune in to their truest needs and you serve them and regard them with a servant heart.

"But your heart itself, is much more mysterious than this. It is so deep. It is so profound and has incredible depths that you need to personally explore, understand, and embody. You have delved deeply into the Celtic Christian Tradition, and you have found that its spirituality and wisdom resonates with you fully. Is it okay if we spend some time now and travel into to the depths to open your heart?"

"Of course" Lyra replied. "I am listening. I'm listening with my whole heart!" She felt a noticeable shiver run through her. Her skin went all prickly with gooseflesh. Her heart started beating faster, as with an adrenalin rush. *This is indeed a unique experience. I am actually talking to a scholarly fish! My capacity for disbelief, is once again being precariously suspended. Hmmmmm . . . .*

She calmed down when she remembered that Bradn *had* introduced himself with these humble words "I am a mystical being." This helped her make some sense of the reality of it all, and to accept his invitation to listen further.

"Watch me for a moment!" Bradn spoke excitedly. He abruptly dove straight down into the depths of the well, disappearing out of sight. He was gone for close to a minute, and Lyra became fidgety. Instead of remaining standing where she was on the muddy and grassy edge of the well, she walked around to the raised rocky edge and bent over to peer into the depths. Feeling a little unsafe there at the edge, she knelt down on the rock, and continued to peer.

Lyra could see a barely perceptible flash of light in the depths, followed by a glimmer and then a vertical line of light. She detected, movement, flow—possibly a current?

Within seconds, this vertical line of light was a broadening trail of iridescent and effervescent light, and she realized that this was actually Bradn accelerating to the surface.

And a few seconds later with a climactic whoosh, Bradn soared into the air high above the well, and he flipped and twisted around so freely, gleefully. Kerploosha! He made a grand splash, landing in the water precisely where he had first exited. The large, perfectly concentric ripples emanated once again, growing ever larger at the edges.

"Look at the ripples" Bradn called out when he reached the surface once again. "Look at them all! They're still there. They're still coming. They weren't there before, and now that I've gone to the depths and back again, there is a marvelous ripple effect." Lyra stretched out her left hand, to the watery surface. She felt the repeating pulse of the ripples. Soft. Strong. Full. Real.

"The ripples are reaching out from the center to the edge of the well, to the mud and to the grass, to the rock, to the air, to you, to anything they can touch or reach. They are there in the moment and they are there to be shared. I want you to hold onto this image for a long time."

Bradn glided over to Lyra's side of the well. As excited as he was to teach Lyra, he was compelled to speak very calmly and rationally, to allow the very essence of the lesson to enter Lyra's perceptibly opening heart.

"Wisdom is like these ripples. Wisdom comes from the depths of the unknown, up into the Light. It brings Light with it. It creates a force, or an energy, in the form of ripples. Wisdom transforms into knowledge for all to learn from, grow from, apply, and embody and share." Bradn paused. "Are you still with me Lyra?"

Lyra nodded receptively. The image of wisdom as an emergence of Light in the deep dark depths, and its transformation into shareable, tangible ripples of knowledge, was so poetic. So real. So very perceptive.

"Bradn," she said "You've just painted a wonderfully memorable and relevant image on my heart. You have a way with imagery and teaching. Thank you!"

Bradn grinned. "I am a Celtic Salmon. I have surely led a most mystical life—a mythical life at that. And I've been diving into the deepest wells of purest sage wisdom throughout my long long life."

He continued "Ancient Celtic folktales from Scotland and Ireland, were passed down through generations, and they all tell of my living in the ancient wells, and of my eating hazelnuts. Hazelnuts were said to be mythical nuggets of wisdom which fell from the hazel trees into the wells.

"Innumerable tales of my special inner wisdom were shared in the oral tradition through story telling. And then they were eventually written down in collections of fables.

"My wisdom, as the Celtic folktales would tell, was shared with others in many unique ways—through the actual hands-on touching of my ripples in the well and through the mere touching of my silvery scales. And, picture this! Through the fine-dining ingestion of a pan-fried serving of me! Ouch! Those who ate me became wise!"

Bradn let out an elongated stream of bigger air bubbles as he chuckled a contemptuous guffaw. Lyra smiled.

Bradn still had more to say. "We all have deep wells of wisdom within us. And we contemplatives are just ordinary folks until we rise up and voice with conviction the words that stir us in our hearts, that stir us in our faith, that stir us in the depths of our souls.

"Then, through our Light, our ripples, our wisdom, our voice, we articulate our honest truths—our depths. We become known for the clarity and the wisdom of our own evocative words.

Deep Diving

"But, getting back on track to the very heart of my teaching, this is my message: I want you to open your heart by learning to deep dive into your own inner well of inherent wisdom. It is truly there in your own depths. You just need time to go there and to dwell there and to return to the surface with the wisdom of the ages—with the wisdom of the inner sage of your soul—with the knowledge of the River flowing and the Lovelight glowing within you. You know things. You intuit things. Wisdom is deep within you.

"Open your heart to God *of whom* you were made. And once you understand this completely and embody these truths, your heart will have such a capacity, like you've never known before. Simply being a loving, caring, compassionate person is deep in itself, but growing and transcending out of the depths of your own inner well of wisdom, well, this is Holy. Wholesome transcendence in its finest. One more step in your journey toward shining brightly—one more step toward becoming most fully human."

Lyra's heart was full and her eyes were wide wide open, almost trance-like, as Bradn looked up at her from the surface of the water.

"I'm going to practice deep diving like you, Bradn! I want to intuit more Sacred truth and wisdom in the depths of my being. I want to discover "the Celtic way of seeing and knowing" that rests deep in my heart and soul. I want to listen for and discern the truths of all time—the Sacred truths that dwell in my deepest depths—beyond the River.

"I'm feeling drawn to the Light beyond the River. I want to experience the River and the Light, as you have! May I be shaped and formed by the Sacredness of my soul—by this deepest well of wisdom within me. May I sense and comprehend the Sound of the Eternal within me.

"Let wisdom arise in me, let wisdom grace me, body mind and spirit. Let wisdom outflow abundantly from my depths, that my presence, my being and my becoming may all be deemed worthy of the Light inherent within me. Then may I send out the shimmering ripple effects to broadly share this Sacred inborn deeper wisdom, for the good of all life here on earth. I offer up a hushed and heartfelt Amen."

Lovelight

Lyra added "I've been calling The River my muse, for a very long time. And I've written about The Lovelight for years. 'Lovelight' is my word for all the gifts that come to me from God—love, joy, hope, peace, grace, strength, wisdom, insight, and courage, and more. Lovelight shines upon me and also glows from deep within me. Lovelight is mystically, intangibly tangible!"

And then her own mystical prose arose from her memory and from her faithful depths. She delighted in speaking its truth out loud by the still water well, as Bradn listened intently. She straightened up to speak and offered these prayerful words. Her voice was clear. Her cadence ever-free:

"God's Holy Lovelight is the very essence—
of the Sacred—
of the Sacred in me—
of the Light in my body, mind and spirit—
of my very being—of my very soul.
Within the Lovelight, through the Lovelight, and in the Lovelight,
the spaciousness
of my heart, and of my consciousness, and of my interconnectedness,
knows no boundaries.
God's Holy Lovelight is my inner Light
my energy, my aura, my essence,
my shimmering luminescence. Amen."

She continued, "I've lately come to regard my poetic Lovelight as a second very stirring muse of mine. So there will be no difficulty, whatsoever for me, to hold up both The River and The Lovelight as my inspirational muses. These will most surely lead to the greater depths of inner wisdom and truth within me."

Bradn smiled. He felt honored to be in her presence as she affirmed her Sacred essence—her Sacred depths. He acknowledged the power and the truth of her words. In his deferential demeanor, he slowly drifted away from Lyra at the rocky edge, and let go a few more tiny bubbles in a trail of glistening luminescence. His silvery iridescence was quite fiery now. He had come to Lyra to share his message. Lyra's heart was open to his wisdom. Her heart was overflowing with the ripples of vibrantly dancing living waters. His work was done.

Into the depths of the ancient well he slipped away, leaving Lyra by the edge on the rock. In that moment, Lyra was in a very good place.

The Word of God

In Real Time—In Prayer

My Child,
I have searched you, I know everything you do,
when you rise, when you lay down,
I am with you.
I know your words and I know your ways.
I know your heart, My Child. Amen.

Through Forest and Trees
Meet Xavad—the Celtic Deer

Around me stands the great central grove—of forest lore and clime—
So palpable the Presence is—serenity divine.
Surrounded now in liminal space—on thresholds of my faith—
Where Holiness pervades my being—delights my tender Faith.

Always Changing, Never the Same

Lyra eventually looked up to the pretty summer sky, as if to see the sun through the dark green coniferous forest canopy. Only tidbits of blue sky were visible, but it was still very bright. Lyra estimated it was close to 5 p.m.

There was just enough of a breeze that Lyra did not feel closed-in by the forest. She reminded herself of some of her previous hikes into the forest, where all was so placid that she had felt she had strayed into the stillness of a wee hollow, or a small dell. Or, quite possibly, she had spiritually segued into a mystical dimension! But not so, on this occasion. She knew that in that moment, she was physically and exquisitely mentally present.

She stood still and took in a long slow breath, in the wandering waft of the wind. She felt the vastness of the forest. It was comfortable. She tuned into the wideness of forest life, and the intricacies and inter-connectedness of all living things in the forest.

Kirk Wipper had taught her another awareness perspective a very long time ago. He had said, "The purest and simplest truth is that there would never, ever be any two moments exactly alike in life. Never. Because all 'life moments' are always evolving, always 'becoming'. Breeze blowing by. Insects buzzing around. Light filtering and warming. Ever-changing patterns of light and shadow on rocks and rivers, and trees. Waxing, waning airborne whiffs of pine-treed forest, fresh aromas of loamy earth, freshwater scents of the nearby stream, faint tang of decaying pine cones and pine bark debris everywhere. 'Always changing, never the same.'" Lyra stood there still, in awe of Creation and the simplest reality—in awe of Kirk's most memorable and meaningful words. She tuned back in to the moment at hand. *This moment is here, and then it is gone, never to be again. It is good, to be in the moment, to live in the moment, to cherish this moment.*

The forest was active and alive and well. It was seething with perpetual renewal. It was resplendent with the natural colors and curves of life. Naturally catalytic, it was supercharged by the powers of earth wind, water and Light.

The Fall

Lyra's eyes were wide open to the culture and the pace of the forest. On her rugged nature walk, she was in a state of heightened awareness and awe of the sights and sounds and scents around her, when misfortune struck.

How ironic is it that someone can tune in so intensively with one's surrounding and still trip over a raised rocky ledge on the path? How could one be *so* intentionally present in the moment, yet *so* obviously absent, all at the same time?

Well, Lyra did just that! While her strong long legs were striding out along the pine needle path, her right toes, in her hiking shoe, failed to clear a two-inch high, sharply-raised, rocky ledge. She struck the rock hard with her toe, causing her whole body to violently pitch, face forward. She was falling quickly toward the rocks and she desperately flailed both of her arms, trying to regain her balance, trying to stay on her feet. Futile. Before she actually fell to the ground, she twisted abruptly to the right, wrenching her body to grab onto a sturdy pine tree trunk just off the path. Her momentum was so great that when she wrapped her arms around the tree, she literally spun around the tree. She slid to an unscheduled sit-in on the ground.

Her head was spinning. Her mind was racing. *What just happened?! How did this happen?! One minute I was walking and the next minute I was barreling toward the earth!* She was exhilarated, and somewhat amused. She had a wild and invigorating adrenalin rush! Her mind was slowly catching up to her body.

She mentally recounted all the sequences of her fall, recognizing the potential danger that the fall was, or could have been. She had never been injured on any of her hikes in the woods, and she didn't want to start now!

She knew that she did not strike her head, and she was thankful for this. She carefully checked the range of motion of her neck, shoulders, elbows, and wrists and discovered they were all fine. She chuckled to herself knowing that her emergency training was kicking in, and she was systematically giving herself a thorough head-to-toe trauma assessment! Not even a splinter on her exposed wrists and hands. She was lucky.

Looking down at her feet, and with great dismay, she noted a really big problem. Upon impact with the sharp rock ledge, her right hiking shoe had split! Exploded on impact! The body of the shoe was actually now separate from the sole, except for a one-inch area around the heel. The sole of her shoe was gaping downward from her foot when she lifted it off of the ground.

Strength of a Braid

Oh, this is terrible! I cannot lose my shoe! I need two shoes to continue on this rugged forest trail! She raised and lowered her right foot a few more times, to watch carefully how the sole was moving independently of rest of the shoe.

I have to find a way to secure this sole, to either the shoe or to my foot. It will be treacherous to be a Shoeless Joe out here, and walking barefoot is just not an option. I'll have to "MacGyver" something, to make this shoe safe. Darn it! Where's the duct tape when you need it, or the crazy glue? Or even some nylon thread on a spool? I'd use my hair scrunchie, but it's way too small. Hey! And just where are those magical forest-dwelling, leprechaun cobblers when I need them? She chuckled.

What reeds or plants would the indigenous folks have used to fix their moccasin? Strips of leather wound around their foot? Tall reedy grasses from the meadow? Braided reeds from the streams and rivers? Hmmmmm . . . . She recalled now, the wonder of the words from the Ecclesiastes 4:12, which inferred that "three" strands in a braided cord were stronger together, than one strand alone. Her mind turned briefly to her beautiful braided bracelet, her lost Celtic braid. Her nana's gift. She sighed in sadness.

What can I braid? A long flexible vine would be great, but this is Canadian Shield region, not the Niagara Escarpment vineyard region! Hey! What about my shoelace? It's right here in front of me and it could be just the answer to my problem! It's already machine-braided, and it is synthetically strong. I wonder if I can take the super-long super-strong shoelace out of the grommets, and use it to bind my sole and shoe together? Hey, Lyra, ol' girl, you got this!

Lyra remained seated on the forest floor, and removed her right shoe and shoelace. While she wound the lace around and around her foot, prayerful words came. "Thank you God for not letting me get hurt when I fell down. Thank you for being present to me on this lovely nature walk. Thank you for keeping me safe, always. You are indeed, everywhere. You are in the wind and in the sun and in the water and in the forest free. You are in every living creature that lives on this earth. You are even in that treacherous ledge of a rock that tripped me up! All of life is Holy, because all of life, is of You."

Graced by Lovelight

Lyra paused for a moment, looked away from her laces, and focused up into the spaces between the lofty pine branches. She could see a multitude of fine radiant sunbeams reaching down toward her through the trees. What a sight! A golden translucence. She was bathed in a glowing pyramid of sparkling, shimmering light. God's Holy Lovelight graced her as she sat unceremoniously on the ground in prayer. She didn't move. She tuned into the mystery and the grace of that Lovelight moment, and she felt calm, uplifted, and held, in that moment. She felt sure and safe in God's ever-presence, there and then.

She was sure that, no matter what, all would be well and that she would journey safely, for God was with her. She spoke out loud, closing her prayer. "Thank you God for the gift of your ever-presence. Thank you for the blessed gift of your comforting Holy Lovelight. Amen."

Trekking with Angus

Lyra now focused her attention on binding her sole and shoe to her foot. She first made a stopper knot right at the end of the long lace, and then fed it through a grommet on the top of her shoe. She then firmly wound the whole lace around, and over and under her foot, securing all three parts. When there were only five inches left, she fed the end of the lace through another grommet and tied a safety knot tightly, right by the grommet. *Take that, MacGyver!*

Lyra was a force to be reckoned with. She was proud of herself for this makeshift repair, but she knew that the moment of truth would come when she stood and took a few steps. *I'm going to have to concentrate on my walking now, and be careful to consciously pick up my foot high enough with each step so as not to get caught up on anything on this trail.*

She took a few careful steps and noted that the lace held well. She took a few more strides and was relieved that it didn't feel like the lace was slipping. She dusted herself off of pine needles and forest debris from her impromptu sit-in on the forest floor.

She also noted for the first time that her right great toe was tender. Not throbbing or wrenching pain, as in a possible fractured toe, but simply a little pain, to remind her of her unexpected toe-stubbing adventure. *A little pain to remind me to be careful on my journey. Time to move on. So much more to see!*

Lyra walked onward on the trail with caution. The lace was doing its job. The trail was leading her through denser underbrush, so she kept her foot-wits about her. It was a little darker as she walked away from her Lovelight moment. She realized that the pine branch canopy was becoming much thicker there, preventing all of the sunrays from reaching her.

Something then struck her funny bone and she laughed out loud. She had a really good belly laugh on the forest path. *I started this walk today, because of WB Yeats's poetic character, named Wandering Aengus, and here I am engineering my shoe repair in the woods, with Angus MacGyver! How lucky can I be—two handsome Anguses for me! Or, would that be two Angii? Or perhaps, Angus was also the plural form?* She laughed at her grammatical query in the middle of a summer's day. She knew that her nitpicking brain—her detail-oriented brain—was clearly working overtime. *Did it really even matter anyway? Angus, Anguses, or Angii?*

Eventually, Lyra was humming. No words. Just humming. The trail varied between smooth exposed rock, pine needle beds, and some jagged weather-worn edges of embedded rock. In time, her humming became a recognizable melody, and her own footsteps set up the rhythm for the tune. She realized that she was now singing the popular secular song about being "raised up"—on mountains, on seas, on shoulders.

"Wow," said Lyra softly. "Words describing the power and the grace of God are beautifully embedded in so many popular songs. I feel like God has lifted me up today, to conquer my shoeless shenanigans, to give me hope and strength and confidence just when I needed it. I feel so blessed to have a faith that gets me through the tough times, one that leads me on to the Light. I feel God-with-me."

Lyra then recalled a hymn based on Psalm 91. The lyrics danced through her mind, again alluding to being raised up, but on eagles' wings. In this very moment, Lyra genuinely felt held and safe—raised up by the grace of God.

Over the next hour or so, Lyra continued her journey, having to stop twice to meticulously rebind her shoe. Her repair was good, but it was not perfect, for the rough terrain was winning. This made Lyra worry, but her optimistic and hopeful nature chased away those fears, and she trekked onward.

Chance Meeting

On the third time when the lace loosened and she had to stop, she sat down on a large flat rock. The rock felt warm to the back of her bare thighs. There was no direct sunlight there early in the evening, yet there was still a warmth, a thermal heat-glow from within the rocks. Nature never ceased to amaze her.

Lyra lingered on the rock and entered into a few moments of life-giving stillness and wonder. She attuned to the energetic bevy of forest life that surrounded her. Again, so many birdsongs! Happy sounds. Cheerful, chirping everywhere. She could easily identify the cardinal's sound. It was clear and distinct. It was the Canadian Acclaimed Avian Vocalist Royale!

Remaining seated with her broken shoe off her foot, she worked away at securing her shoe-fix. The knot itself was slipping and the braid was gradually loosening around her shoe. She persevered in her work.

She heard something in the distance. *Sounds like laughter! I rarely ever meet anyone out here, especially in this deeply wooded section. Most hikers go in as far as the stream or the waterfalls or even the well, but I can't recall any chance meetings with folks here in the deeply-wooded coniferous forest.*

She sat still, listening, and sure enough, she heard the laughter again. Gleeful. Exuberant. Belly laughter. Hahaha laughter. She turned her face toward the sound. And there, seventy-five feet away on the trail, just climbing up over the crest of a large, sloping rock, were two people hiking. Actually, a man and a woman. *A man and a teenager!* Both were wearing knapsacks she noted, as they approached. A fit-looking middle-aged man and an energetic youth were striding out on a hike together, on a glorious warm August day.

"Paul! Saint Paul Almighty!!" she called out in recognition of the man.

"Lyra! Selfless Saint Lyra!" he answered back. "What happened? Are you okay? Why are you barefoot in the middle of the forest?"

Lyra laughed and simply said "Thanks, Paul. I'm okay! Really, I'm fine! No need for a visit to the Emergency Department today! I take it that this lovely young lady is your daughter Crea—I haven't seen her for a couple of years now!" She said to Crea "You are so tall, and so grown up now, young lady! Look at you! You're as tall as me now! Are you enjoying this beautiful weather? It's so nice to have this sunshine after all the rains we had last week."

Crea smiled. She remembered meeting Nurse Lyra many times at the hospital where her dad worked. In her childhood, she had often spent her Saturday mornings in the ER, just to be near her dad while her mom got errands and shopping and stuff done in town. She could picture Lyra always taking time with the little children in the ER, making sure they were happy and not scared. She had many fond memories of Lyra, and she liked her a lot.

"I think the last time I saw you, Lyra, was when you brought your puppy, Paidi over to play with our new puppy, Jovi. They rolled around and played like silly pups. They were so funny together. Jovi is ten pounds now. How big is Paidi? How IS Paidi?"

"Oh, she's still pretty tiny, just a wee six pounds of pure love."

Crea said with delight. "It's my birthday today! I'm fourteen! So, we're out for a daylong hike. My choice! We're halfway around the trail. The best part is just up ahead."

Crea continued, "I love going in to the waterfalls. Right in under the falls. It's the best fun of all! It's worth the hike to get there. People in the big cities don't get to just walk away from their homes and climb in under a waterfall like this! This is great! I'm sooooo lucky!"

Paul responded. "Crea, my darling little teenager, when did you grow up so fast? Since when did you become such an old soul?"

Crea said mysteriously. "Maybe there is something in the water here, Dad! Haha! You do know about the legends!"

Lyra smiled. Crea was so right. The legends told of the powers of the waters of the River Saye, that there was something sage about the waters. There was much to reverence in the water and in the air near the Saye. She said out loud "Maybe we'll all become the wise ones? Maybe we'll all shine brightly into our tomorrows with wisdom. So the legends say. May it be so!"

Lyra reminded herself that Crea was only fourteen. She knew that Crea was only being playful in her words about the legends, but Lyra could see, as could Paul, that Crea had grown up. Solid. Savvy. Sage. Crea was experiencing nature, allowing nature shape her, body mind and spirit. Lyra felt contented in knowing this—in seeing this firsthand.

"Does your dad go in under the waterfalls too?" Lyra asked.

Crea looked at her dad. Paul smiled and said "No I don't go under the falls. Someone has to be the lifeguard, and that's me. The rocks are really mossy and slippery in there, and it wouldn't do if both of us slipped and fell, or worse."

Lyra smiled. She could hear the voice of reason in Paul's fatherly tone. She could feel the strength of his safety-first stance in his words.

Crea chimed in. "But I don't like wearing my hiking boots in the stream and in the falls. If I did, I'd have to wear wet squishy hiking boots all the way home. And that's pretty yucky. So I have a second pair of shoes. Crocs, in my knapsack. I'll put them on when I get to the waterfall".

She paused. "How come you took your shoe off out here, Lyra? And why are the laces off?"

And before Lyra could even answer, Paul called out "She blew a shoe! Look at it Crea! What on earth did you do Lyra, to destroy your shoe?"

Lyra recounted her recent fall, and her self-assessment for injury, and then she told of her jury-rigging the shoe.

Paul laughed "You're such an independent woman! Always the problem solver. You always came up with just the right solutions in the ER—and even out here in the woods. For sure, Angus MacGyver would be proud!"

Sasquatch and Cinderella

Crea laughed with them, and then realized that she, personally, had the perfect solution for Lyra's predicament. "Lyra, would you like to borrow my Crocs for the rest of your hike? You need a pair of shoes for hiking, way more than I need them for playing!"

She looked over at her dad, who nodded in approval. His teenager was growing up quickly. She was sensible, perceptive, and sensitive. She was able to work through situations with a level head and clear insight.

He smiled proudly. "Yes Lyra, take Crea's Crocs. They're sturdier than your makeshift shoelace binding. And maybe just once, I'll let Crea play in the waterfall barefoot. Maybe just this once!"

Lyra was silent. She was moved at the girl's simple offer of sharing shoes. She was even more moved that she had bumped into fellow hikers, who just happened to have a second pair of shoes on hand, just when Lyra needed them!

"I'm afraid to ask, Crea, what size shoe do you wear? Maybe yours won't fit my feet."

Crea answered, "Size 10, but don't tell anyone that I have such big feet. OMG, I'm embarrassed to even say the size!"

Lyra gasped "I just cannot believe this! That's my shoe size too! I have bigger feet than I like too. That's amazing that you have just what I need!"

Paul laughed, his eyes were dancing "If the shoe fits, wear it! Haha! Oh, hey Lyra! Should I start calling you Cinderella?"

Lyra laughed too, and said "This forest will never ever be the same—a sighting of TWO Bigfoots in one day. For sure, we'll all have a Sasquatch tall tale or two to share someday, back in town!"

Lyra felt suddenly warm all over, as Crea reached for her knapsack and handed over the lime green Crocs. "Dad tells me to wear the strap behind my ankle, for safety's sake."

Lyra laughed. "Of course Saint Paul, I'll wear the strap behind my ankle. These Crocs will be so much safer than my broken, beat-up hiking shoe. Crea, can I give you a really big hug? You have just made my day!"

Crea held out her arms to receive, and to give, a warm, hold-me-tight hug, the kind that kids often give to folks they know and trust.

Lyra cherished the tenderness of the moment and then she stood back. She put on the very loudly lime-colored shoes, and they fit! They fit well enough to go a-traipsing and a-trekking through the woods. They didn't even hurt her sore right toe. *Perfect. Life is good*!

Lyra said to Crea "These shoes really aren't lime green, Crea. In my mind they are golden. Pure gold!"

Crea laughed, and took the bait. "Hey Lyra, I remember the fairy tales about ruby slippers and glass slippers. Hahaha! Maybe we'll make up our own story about the golden Crocs!"

Paul joined in "Whoa, ladies. Hold on a minute! Golden Crocs? That's a bunch of crock! No one in their right mind will ever believe you!"

"We'll make them believe us, Paul! Just you wait! Crea and I will write a fairy tale or a children's book, with a great moral to the story! Start thinking about that now, Crea! We can have some great fun with this together, down the road!"

"Crea said "Yeah, that would be cool. Maybe this story will be famous like other golden fairy tales—'Rumpelstiltskin', or 'The Goose Who Laid the Golden Egg'! Maybe we'll call ours 'The Magic of the Golden Crocs!' We need a villain and a plot—and a golden superpower! We need some shady characters. Whoohooo, I can't wait to get started!"

"You're off to an amazing start Crea. Maybe in a couple of weeks, I'll bring Paidi over to play with Jovi, and we'll see what you've come up with by then!"

"I like that idea a lot." Crea grinned. "Lyra, you always have great ideas. Your church children's plays are really funny, but they always mean something more. This will be fun to write together. Thanks, Lyra!" They shared in another warmhearted hug.

Lyra spent a moment to tie her two hiking shoes together in a circular fashion, and hung them over one shoulder, like a pair of skates. She could therefore continue hiking, hands-free. *Even though these shoes are now totally worthless, I'll still pack them out of the woods. Leave no trace.*

"We should move on." said Paul. "I'm glad we bumped into you today. Perfect timing! Win. Win. Have a great hike Lyra. See you in town sometime! Just drop the shoes off at the ER someday and I'll make sure Crea gets them".

"Bye" said Lyra. "Give Jovi a big squeeze for me! Say 'hi' from Paidi too! Happy Birthday Crea! Have a great time at the waterfall! And thanks so very much—you are my very own magical shoe-fixin' leprechaun and my benevolent friend of the forest today!" They smiled and moved on.

Praise and Prayerful Psalm

Lyra's heart was full. Her mind began erupting with a praise song, and she knew she wanted to break out and sing. Instead, she simply said in the quiet forest sanctuary "Praise God! Always and ever, praise God!"

Lyra's God was awesome. "God is good—always. And always, God is good." More words of conviction and faith were tumbling forth out of Lyra. She really enjoyed taking the time to praise her God, in the big and in the little moments of her daily living.

And then some very dear words came to her tongue. These were sentiments in the format of Psalm 23, but they were written in modern day language. Lyra could recite these words by heart, as she herself had written them, back in 2008, when she had been musing deeply on the treasured psalm.

She walked along attuning to the beauty all around her. She was aware of the glow of Holy Lovelight there in the forest midst, and still even more cognizant of the timely provision of God's help in her dark valley, in her time of need. She spoke these words in a reverent voice, with a thankful heart, and with a deepest affirmation of her own and very real, living faith:

A Lovelight 23rd

The Kindest Shepherd is my Gentle Pastor
With him, I want for nothing at all.
I'll seek and search no more.
He makes sure that I come into stillness, that I rest.
He shows me the warmth of his peace and calm.
He brings Light to my soul.
His Holy Lovelight stills me, heals me, and makes me whole.
He tells me his way, and I choose the right pathways on my journeys.
And in the depths, and in the darkest times of my journey,
I'll not be afraid—nor will I worry.
For you God, my Kindest Shepherd, are with me.
Your very Presence brings me comfort. You quiet my restless heart.
You lift me up—You raise me up amidst the unbelievers. You freely give to me.
You gift me with the wonders of your abundance and your blessings.
I believe that your loving-kindness will grace me,
in your Holy Lovelight, through all of my earthly days.
And I will walk with you, my Gentle Pastor,
hand in hand—heart in heart—One-with-you forever.
I will journey in the Living Faith—in your Holy Lovelight—forever, Amen.

She knew, and felt, that God had been with her throughout the day. Call it luck or call it God's provision, she was wholly comforted in experiencing simultaneously and firsthand, both the Provision of God and the Presence of God. *God is good!*

Slant, Shape and Shade

Lyra continued to walk in her mindfulness of God. She questioned the validity, and to some extent the reality, of some current church vocabulary. Wonderfully weighted words like presence, eternal and eternity, omnipotence, abundance, callings, spiritual nudgings, mystics, prophesy, higher ground and Holy Ground, Oneness, Sacredness, Holiness—these were all expressions over which she had previously pondered in her woodland walks. She found great joy in affirming her new understandings. She had a newfound comfort, relevance and place, for all of these words and concepts. They were real for Lyra.

She had also, over time, chewed away at some harder words—darker words—those which she found to be void of any personal draw or inspiration whatsoever. For the biblical words Lord and Lordship, King and Kingdom, power, authority, dominion and reign, Lyra had tried hard to find any positive meaning or application for these words, for herself individually and collectively for the diverse cultures in the modern world. But, she just couldn't.

She didn't need her God to be a King, or a Lord, with authority, dominion and powers over her. She preferred her God to be all-knowing, wise, approachable and ever-present. A friend and a confidante. Loving, and gently leading. She felt comfortable in trusting and obeying a loving, fatherly God. So she simply ceased to use the dark words in her spoken and written vocabulary. She also avoided using negative words—war-themed words—army and armor, battle blood and conquest, vanquish, victory foes, and supremacy.

Lyra's was a peaceable soul. And, like the renowned monk, Brother Lawrence of the seventeenth century, she had learned and mastered "Practicing the Presence of God", a practice that would shape her ongoing spiritual formation in a most personal and intimate way.

Lyra thought about her own church, then. She was raised in the United Church of Canada. She had always admired the openness of the UCC in responding to questions of the faith and the doctrine. Her heart was warmed by the sensitive directions it had taken—and was taking—toward inclusive-ness. She appreciated her denomination's ability to embrace all forms of diversity in this country and world, a wonderful modern mosaic of life and living. She approved of her church's nationwide leadership in all matters concerning Indigenous Truth and Reconciliation processes. Transparency and openness and humility were key in all T&R conversations.

And, Lyra's own family members—her extended family—had also had a hand in sculpting her personhood and her faith. Her mom, dad, older sister, and all four grandparents played key roles in coloring, sketching, and shading, the vibrant dimensionality of Lyra's being. Her perspectives, her stance, and her luminous depths were all natural fallouts of her family's influence, of their reach and their hold and their wholesome truths. Their respective deep wells of wisdom rippled their way into Lyra's life and faith with subtlety and with grace. Their ripple effects were mystical. Her ances-tral draw was strong, magnetic, her true north.

Lyra's bestimal life, her best life and the essence of her being were a living testament to the familial voices of the past, the sage voices of the ages, and the voice(s) of the Eternal. She connected with the many voices of wisdom and truth anchored deep within her. Life was good.

Called by Name, Known, and Understood

The trail began to lead her down a large sloping, smooth rock. She saw some movement farther down the slope. She stopped and stayed still for a moment, hoping to catch sight of the mover. There was a hush in the forest. Seeing no more movement, she remained perfectly still. In anticipation, she kept a watchful eye.

She honed in on a more subtle movement through the brush at the base of the smooth rock slope. She melted in awe at what she saw. A fam-ily of deer was walking together. Mama was with a gangly wee Bambi at her side, and Papa was just ahead of them, with his stately rack of antlers crowning his grand masculine physique. Lyra's human scent had alerted them, and caused them to stop in their tracks.

Papa turned his head, and nodded slowly at Mama, who then walked slowly and surely, with measured precision and grace, around behind a larger rock. Mama was leading her Bambi out of direct sightline, away from Lyra. Without a sound, Papa had sent his family to safety, while he stood watch and observed Lyra's movements.

Lyra and Papa made direct eye contact. Just down the slope from each other, they were only about fifteen feet apart. For Lyra, this was a beautiful moment, to be cherished. It is a rare occasion when humans can actually get close enough to make eye contact with wildlife. In her stillness, she watched, listened, and opened her whole self to the minutiae of the moment. The hush was unmistakably still there. Not a cricket, nor a buzzing bee, nor even a chirping birdsong interrupted it.

Unexpectedly, Papa lowered his head gently, bringing his antlers down in front of his lowered head. *Is he going to charge at me? Am I safe?*

No sooner had she thought these things, when Papa slowly raised his head up. He was still watching her intently, and he spoke with a deep bass voice, in kindly, dulcet tones.

"Hi Lyra, my name is Xavad! I was hoping to spend some time with you on your journey today. I have lots to tell you!"

Lyra relaxed. She lowered herself to sit on the downward sloping rock, extending her long legs out fully. *Oh, it's so good to be off my feet and to just stretch out for a few minutes!* She no longer felt any potential dangers. Her mind was racing though, with curiosity. *This is the fourth creature of the woodlands, who actually knows me, and has called me by my name!*

"Well hello Xavad! And it's my great pleasure to meet you too! I'm sorry if I disturbed your family. I'm not here to hurt anyone or anything. I hope you'll let them know that they are safe. They can come out of hiding, if you'll let them. I am intrigued, that you know my name! I am fascinated by your comment, that you "have lots to tell me." I have so many questions for you!" Lyra's voice trailed off.

"Lyra, I have been watching you from afar, throughout your journey today. I am fascinated, with how your tenacity and determination have helped you to conquer your shoe-related setbacks. I sense that your stead-fastness and your perseverance and your veritable spunk all stem from something very deep in your soul. Do you follow me? Do you know what I'm talking about?"

Lyra replied, very superficially "Oh yes, everyone who knows me, calls me the eternal optimist or the positive one. Someone else once said I was relentless in getting the job done. Maybe that's a good thing, I guess. I just chalk it up to just gittin' 'er dun! A little intestinal fortitude and a little personal resolve can go a long way in accomplishing any task. Sometimes a little creative thinking is helpful too." She remembered her braided shoe-lace binding, and she smiled inwardly. She also realized, that her words and thoughts were rambling, rolling, and tumbling along—again. She consciously stopped herself, and chose instead to just listen.

"Yes, Lyra, that is all true, but I see so much more than this, and I hope to help you to see it too. I believe, that deep down within you is a rock-solid faith that buoys you up and bolsters you up and helps you to face the situations at hand with grace, integrity, courage, and of course, with ingenuity! Your faith is central to your very being, and it is through the strength of your faith, that you can move forward with confidence, with purpose and with vision, in all circumstances."

He continued in his lesson "Your faith permeates everything about you, like a river running through your very being. And this gives you an innate stick-to-it-ness and conviction. You Lyra, have been gifted generously with the grace of God, and that has brought you along on a lifelong journey in the Living Faith!" Xavad opened his mouth and grinned quite broadly, showing his enormous yellowed teeth. In the greatness of this message, he slowly, slowly, stretched his massive head back, tilting his grand rack of antlers backward to touch his back. He was relaxed and comfortable in Lyra's company.

Lyra had been watching Xavad. She too was enjoying his company, his words, and his calm in the moment. She asked him with great coiling curiosity "How is it that you can see the depth of my faith? How can you tell that the deepest roots of my true grit are centered in my deep faith?"

Xavad looked into her eyes intently, with a softness that authenticated his genuine interest in Lyra's understanding. "Lyra, I am a Celtic mystical deer. We deer are recognized through many cultures and mystical traditions, to be highly spiritual beings. We are not deities per se, but so much of ancient lore and mythology is laced with stories of our great spiritual intuition, and our spiritual wisdom. We approach creatures, time and place, on an omniscient level. We intuit. We know. We have intimate sensing and knowledge of all life and living.

"And it is this very realm of spirituality that has me so deeply attuned to the depths of your faith. You already know your God. You are so very aware of God's Presence in your life, and of God's leading in your life. You have even said yourself that you know, personally, what it means to be called by God, when you told your minister, more than a decade ago, that you were being called to serve in a Parish Nursing Ministry.

"You have shown throughout your nursing career, throughout your Compassionate Life, that you have a readiness to serve your God. Indeed, you have a servant heart. You, Lyra, are truly a spiritual being. Through your watchfulness, your willingness to grow in faith, and through your intrinsic grace, you have emerged in your world as a woman of deep faith, with a discerning spiritual connectedness, a woman in touch with her own sacredness and her own sacred pathway."

Xavad watched while Lyra smiled and fondly reminisced over her long life of service, both in the ER and in her short ten years serving as Parish Nurse to her colorfully intergenerational congregation and community. *I have ministered well! I have served well! The Light of my ministry still shines brightly in my heart, in my midst, and in my life. I feel blessed.*

Xavad continued. "Lyra, you have also read extensively about the Celtic Wisdom Tradition, and you have contemplated your own personal place in modern-day Celtic Christianity. You have even begun to state out loud to interested listeners that you were born into and raised in the United Church of Canada, but you now identify with and embody the profound teachings of Celtic Christianity. Even today on your nature walk, you made several references to the inherent Sacredness of all life forms in the forest world, and in the pond world, and in the universal skies. You view the world through the prism lenses of love, compassion and respect. You do see and discern and appreciate the Holiness in all living beings."

Xavad paused to collect his thoughts. Lyra remained attentively silent, eager to hear more.

"Your faith has grounded you Lyra, and has made you whole, more than you even realize. But I'm hoping that you're still with me on this tangent. Please listen carefully.

"You are already familiar with *liminal spaces*—perceived thresholds between *what was*, and *what will be*. Would you agree with me that at this point in your personal journey and in your faith journey you are truly in a liminal space? You have fully retired and left behind an impressive career in nursing, and a lifetime in the Compassionate Life. You have reflected deeply on your future in the Contemplative Life and in the Creative Life. Discernment, prayer, reading, educational retreats, and silent retreats have all been intentional parts of your discernment journey last year. Your actual pace of your spiritual journey has drastically slowed, as you have cautiously looked, listened, sensed, learned, grown and prayed your way to your spiritual maturity. Yours has been a transformative journey.

"Like a deer, you have been methodical. You have intentionally taken your time on your spiritual formation journey, allowing your journey to unfold in its own time. You have been taking baby steps in your faith journey in the name of making well-informed and wholesome choices for your own spiritual health and well-being. Your every step, like ascending the irregular south stairs to the ancient Temple Mount in Jerusalem, is cautious and weighed. You approach God in this same measured way, with diligence and discipline. Your every move, like a deer in the woods, is slow, well thought out, precise, and timely. Would you agree that all of this is true, and accurate for you?"

Lyra was absolutely wide-eyed and speechless. She felt an incredible warmth all through her body, and the heat seemed to concentrate in her heart. She felt encouraged by the warmth, calmed by its presence, intrigued by its energy, and most of all, humbled by its essential grace. She couldn't answer with words, so she subtly nodded in agreement.

"Just a few more things before my big lesson. Lyra, I witnessed many of your instinctive and reverent responses to the events in your day. Before you set out on your hike this morning, you naturally centered yourself by pausing in a quiet prayer, and in silence. And later, when your heart was overflowing with gratefulness, you offered a prayer of thanksgiving to God. When you were burdened with concern for your safety, you asked for God's Presence and safekeeping. When your heart was on fire, elated with joy over God's timely provision of shoes, you praised God in the words of your Psalm. You praised God with great conviction from your soul. There is always an Amen resting on your heart, moving with your soul, floating on your every breath. Your prayer life is one continuous breath of Amen.

"And earlier today, as you learned your important life-lessons from Zoli, Yala, and Bradn, you attuned all of your senses and your awareness to the inherent Holiness of all life in your midst. As Abraham of the Old Testament was clearly the quintessential archetype of faith, so too are you Lyra, that same portrayal in the new millennium!"

Lyra blushed so very intensely at those words. She felt they were far too grand in relation to her humble self. In her reticence, she was about to deflect that last comment. For a fleeting moment, she even considered changing the subject.

But, with grace and dignity and increasing gratitude, she chose to hold onto those powerful words of praise. She nodded, humbly accepting the compliment.

A delightful silence just stood there with them, in their deep forest conversation, suspending Xavad's heartfelt monologue, giving space and time for Lyra to experience yet another light-bearing moment—another Holy Moment—wherein she could appreciate the fullness and the wonder of the Holy in her midst. This weighted silence was golden.

Lyra was moved by Xavad's insight into the depth and the very roots of her inborn faith. A comforting memory drifted into center stage of her conscious thoughts. She recalled meeting with her pastor, early on in the new millennium, after she had had repeated rounds of medical tests, complex procedures, and multiple extensive surgeries. Her spirit was low. She was quite disillusioned with her then current state of ill health, and she was feeling more than a little spiritually drained.

She had said to him "I feel like I'm reaching out in desperation for help, like the woman in the Bible who reached out to touch the hem of Jesus' robe."

Pastor Colin had responded to her words, quoting that very same Scripture found in Luke, saying "You might be feeling that you are reaching out in desperation, but truly, you are reaching out in faith. Lyra, it is actually the power of your faith, which has made you—which is making you—strong." Lyra recalled that in that moment, Colin's gentle voice had suddenly changed. It was quite different. It sounded hollow, muffled, ethereal. Yet still, deeper, grounded and resonant. She then remembered thinking "His voice is like a Holy Voice, in a Holy Moment, in a Holy Place. Like, the voice of God is echoing Pastor Colin's—it is one with Pastor Colin's. Like, God's Presence is being made known to me through the simplest words of Scripture. Like, God is speaking directly into my soul. Like, God is vocally channeling a healing power into my wholly receptive being."

In the present moment, in the deep forest with Xavad, Lyra held onto the comfort of that memory—there, in the Light. She knew in her heart that it was most surely her faith, her persevering and relentless faith, which was keeping her strong, always.

Xavad, took in a big breath, paused, and slowly exhaled. Lyra heard his deep breath, and this reminded her to fill her own lungs fully and completely, bringing oxygen-rich blood to all of her cells and body parts. She exhaled slowly, too. They both remained motionless, he standing, she seated at the base of the sloping rock. *In this moment, I feel spiritually exhilarated. I feel I am truly known, and understood.*

OPEN YOUR FAITH

A few minutes went by when Lyra spoke. "Xavad, you know me well. You know my heart even more than I do. Your awareness of my life, of my journey, is uncanny. It bewilders me. One of my favorite Scriptures, Psalm 139, marvels at the ever-presence of God in our lives. Paraphrased—in short

> "Oh where can I go—if I ascend to heaven—
> if I take the wings of the morning—You God, are ever-there."

Lyra paused, immersing herself in the knowledge of—and in the intimate comfort of—God's ever-presence.

Xavad spoke gently but firmly in a Godlike, fatherly voice "Faith is the assurance of things hoped for, and the conviction of things not seen. And you know this Lyra, for you know your Scriptures well. You embody them through your living faith."

Xavad took another deep breath. "I think I've painted a big enough picture for you. Now it's time for me to teach you. I'm only going to ask one thing of you Lyra, and that is this. Open your faith. Always. And forever. Eternally. Never stop on your faith journey. Always move forward in your becoming more fully human, in your spiritual formation, and in your wholesome transformation. Open yourself to the wonders of the faith, to the vastness and the *veritas* of your open faith. Tune in to the Holiness of every moment. Respect the Sacredness inherent in all of life. Treasure the stories of other faiths, both Eastern and Western and other faith traditions, and realize that they are *all* built upon the profound truths of life and of living. Embody the words "wide open faith". And finally, cherish your own, wide open faith."

Putting it All Together

Lyra knew in her heart that her faith was already wide open. She had eagerly embraced the wonders of Celtic wisdom, even though some teachings clearly clashed with her Christian upbringing. *Is this what Xavad is referring to? Do I need to stretch my faith even more, to question barriers and boundaries and rifts and clashes in doctrine? Do I need to embrace more Eastern and Western interfaith wisdom and history and their spiritual practices? Do I need to allow for more Holy Mystery to rest on my heart?*

Then and there, Lyra recalled a few folks in her life who daily embodied the words wide-open faith—folks who embraced diversity in religious practice—folks who stirred Lyra into expanding her religious boundaries. Her minister's wife Pat, was also a United Church Minister. Her faith had been shaped by great worldly and community faith movements—in China, France, Scotland, Eritrea, and Nicaragua. She was called, in her later ministry, to serve in meaningful social justice ministries. It was Pat's wide-open faith that stirred Lyra into a questing journey into Christlike living. It was Pat's own embodiment of wide-open faith that would bring Lyra into wholeness, completeness, and Oneness with God.

Lyra's Nova Scotian cousin, Rodney, was raised in the Christian household. In his early teaching career, he had experienced the Asian cultures firsthand, while working in Japan as an ESL educator. He dove into the oceans of applied wisdom and practices of the Eastern religions, with inquisitive wonder. At a very young age, he became a sage and centered soul. He was broad-minded, and openly welcoming to both Eastern and Western faith traditions. It was Rodney's wide-open faith that broke through the then rigid boundaries of her tender living faith, in her own young adulthood. She felt newly free to contemplate deeply, on her stirring questions of the faith.

Another young woman, a UK minister's daughter, was moved to literally perform the mysteries. In her Eastern styled lyrical dance, she graced many fringe theatre stages across Eurasia. She took on a wholesome body mind and spirit appreciation of philosophy, metaphysics and transcendent powers of the Eastern religions. Dancing on stage brought her faith forward to her audiences in a most tangible form.

She graced them with an energy, a presence, a Sacredness. She literally lived out—and shared on stage—the mysteries of her merging Eastern and Western Living Faith Traditions. Her own versions of original liturgical dance were profoundly pleasing. That young dancer's wide-open faith was felt, lived, and breathed by all who watched her perform. Her dance tended souls—harkened souls—opened souls—opening all to the promise of a faith flowing into fullness.

Lyra held an exquisite appreciation for both the reach and the depth of the young dancer's faith, as she danced her passions and her beliefs into audiences' hearts. She danced with utmost sensitivity, vulnerability and with whole-body-expressivity. She bonded and connected with her audiences in their shared, wide-open faith journeys.

Lyra reflected pensively, *I wonder where my wide-open faith will lead me? Do I need to dabble more in the East? To crossover from West to East to become transcendently most human? Do I need more study and grounding in the teachings of the ancient mystics? What further wisdom, experience, and faith disciplines do I need, in order to shape my soul, form my faith, carve my convictions, and steer my future studies? How can I literally rest and ride and revel in my river of life and love and learning?*

In response to her own deeper and wider musing, she felt an unusual and powerful pull within her. That pull was a giant magnetic force drawing her strongly toward an unknown direction off of her beaten path. It was like a hunger just hankering to be filled with newness, goodness and vitality. That same pull called her along her spiritual formation journey.

Xavad had been watching Lyra intently as she quietly introspected. It was like he knew her thoughts, and her heart, as she carefully formed each question.

She did not voice any of her specific questions out loud, but she did offer words of gratitude. "Xavad, you are wonderful. Your insights into faith, humanity, and my own personal journeys, are incredible. You have been so present to me, and so helpful in painting an accurate picture of my journey—of my faith. I have such clarity into my own faith journey right now. I will need time to sift through all that you have said, and put it all into meaningful contexts, and purposeful actions in my life."

She closed her eyes, and when she opened them again, Xavad was gone, vanished. Not a trace. No Mama or Bambi either. Silently they had moved on as a family, together in unity, safe in the center of their forest home, leaving Lyra there, in trancelike awe and wonder and bliss.

The Word of God
In Real Time—In Prayer

My Child,
You came in faith, seeking.
You came in faith, believing.
You came in faith, trusting.
Your faith has healed you.
The strength of your faith has healed you.
Go and be well.
Go, and be at peace, My Child. Amen.

In the Clearing
Meet Aorla—the Celtic Dove

Where meadow meets the fair forest edge—where Light and dark do play—
Safe from the storm and all that harms—where I can find my way—
Where cooing sounds of mothering doves fall peaceful on my ears—
Awash I am—my soul ascends. I trust. I'm loved. No fears.

Moving On

Lyra continued on her hike through the dense pine treed forest. The day was still warm. A gentle breeze came up, and to her delight, there were still no mosquitoes! Yay!! Along the way, she touched pine cones. She laid her hands on bark and felt the textures of its scaly whorled patterns. She brought a branch of pine needles close to her nose and breathed in deeply, savoring the rich pine aroma. Her hands became sap-sticky, and every once in a while when the trail came closer to the stream, she would rinse and rub her hands with mud and grit, to rid herself of the tacky gunk.

Fallen pine needles were everywhere, scattered where they fell, or where the wind blew them. Where they were deeply distributed, they created a cushioned path. Where they lay over rock, they created a real potential for skidding. Lyra, in her lime green Crocs, was very wary in her every step, so as not to skid.

The terrain of this deep forest was quite variable. Long stretches of gently winding and level trails, were mixed with abrupt turns, navigating around large rocky outcrops or strewn glacial rocks. There were some gentle changes in elevation on the trail, and some rather steep ascents and descents.

These trails were a few hundred years old, and she reflected on the early settlers of the region, and the indigenous folks who intimately knew the lay of the land. She admired them. They knew the rugged Canadian landscape so well. They lived it. They were one with the land. They were hearty, and hardy. They had a deep respect for the land, for Creation itself, and for all life within Creation. They had trail-blazed their way through life, so that future generations would have a beautiful, accessible, natural place to call home—a home to which they and their ancestors were deeply, inherently connected—a home and a land of their Creator's manifestation and welcomed Presence.

Then, Lyra thought of her new friends of the forest, whom she had met individually earlier in the day. Zoli the dragonfly by the pond. Yala the raven of the wide-open skies. Bradn, the salmon of the ancient well. Xavad, the all-knowing deer of the forest. They all were symbolic creatures who had taken the time to voice their profound messages to Lyra, out of kindness, compassion, and a wide-open love for their world. They lived in trust and in harmony with nature. By teaching their wisdom and by sharing their insights with the human in their midst, they were strengthening their already harmonious relationships.

Lyra smiled fondly as she recounted each message in her mind. She recalled the deep awe and the wonder she felt as they opened her in so many helpful ways. *I'll have to grab my notebook as soon as I get home to write down every morsel of this shared wisdom so I don't forget the details!* She looked forward to musing deeply at home, when the time was right.

This part of her journey was a harder go, due to the rugged nature of the forest topography. She chuckled as she thought *Cartographers would likely curse this terrain in their mapmaking excursions. Plotting shorelines and elevations and creating contour lines to give a 3-D synopsis of the lay of the land—all of this would be highly technical and detailed work. And here I am, blindly trusting while I'm brazenly traipsing in the forest with not even a map or a compass in hand! I've got a lot of nerve I'll say! But, the trail itself has become so visible. It's been so well trodden over the years. Even a novice could walk this trail without any map or compass, and they would still find their way out.*

Her journey through the dense forest was slow. It had been delayed earlier because of frequent stops to re-configure her shoe lacing. She was still so grateful to have Crea's shoes! Lyra had tarried long in her most recent conversations with Paul, Crea, and with Xavad. And, as a result, the day was getting ahead of her.

She turned her head at the sound of the familiar *ho hoo hoo hoododo,* the nocturnal sounds of the great horned owl. She could not locate the large feathered beauty, but she knew by the sound that it was nearby. She was hoping to catch a glimpse of its giant golden eyes—such a stunning sight to see. They would seem to glow by their own light, their own inner light, in the twilight hours. "Hello Mr Owl, my awesome neighborhood owl. Have a lovely evening, my friend." She gave a kindly nod it its general direction. She picked up her pace along the path.

It must be getting close to 9 p.m., as the sun is still lingering just above the horizon in the western sky. The August sun sets much later up north here, and the longer hours of light are most welcomed. Pretty soon, I'll emerge from the depths of the central forest into the bordering deciduous forest, and then onward to the shores of the River Saye.

She looked about, and noted that up ahead, sure enough, the foliage of the trees abruptly changed, from thin coniferous needles to broad deciduous leaves. More sun was able to penetrate the deciduous forest, and at that time of the evening, the longer hazy golden sunrays were nearly horizontal. They sifted through the tree canopy and the tree trunks alike, casting an ambiance of elegance and splendor in the forest. This moment of phenomenal Lovelight lighting brought with it a sense of calm and contentment.

Lyra was embraced by the absolute simplicity surrounding her. She walked along, mesmerized in the golden Light rays. For a few moments, she mused on the word "befriended", for she truly felt she was being befriended by the golden arms of Holy Light.

Befriended

Befriended. Old world morphology in word structure, yet, new world relevance and poetic appeal. Such an interesting word. It was simple, resonant and real. Lyra liked the word. It was a feel-good word. Names and faces of folks who had befriended her in her life, streamed through her mind. She smiled, knowing that she had been supported, strengthened and encouraged—befriended—throughout her whole life by her church, her community and her colleagues. What a lovely sentiment—being befriended!

Then suddenly, her paternal grandfather's face emerged clearly in her mind's eye. Grampie-Chester was a farmer. He was wiry, lean and wizened from hardship and his long hours spent working the land. He was often outwardly gruff. "Grumpie" Lyra would sometimes say. He had a heart of gold and a real soft spot for all of his grandchildren.

Lyra's remembered his hands. Grampie-Chester's hands were giant! Oversized mitts! To Lyra as a young child, they were as large as baseball mitts! But, as large and as strong as they were, his hands were tender, gentle, and loving. They were large with love.

Lyra suddenly understood why her thoughts had moved to Grampie-Chester. His very large hands had befriended her often. Her subconscious was actually choosing his hands, as a symbol of befriending! Holding his hand was like holding a security blanket. His handholding, was connecting and comforting. It was bonding. His tender hold—her tiny child-sized hand in his—meant endearment. It had some built-in nuances of confidence and assurance. Holding Grampie-Chester's hand was an overt act of trust. His hands befriended her soul.

She recalled a tender moment from a long time ago. As a preschooler, she had been walking with her grandfather in the rolling hayfields on the farm in the sunshine. She had instinctively looked upward and reached upward, to hold his rough and weathered hand. His straw hat framed his weather-lined face and the sun haloed his head. He looked down and smiled at her, as they walked together, hand in hand, in the golden Light. The memory was at once poetic and powerful. The memory of his hands, and of his befriending, stilled her soul. What a lovely image to hold onto, there, in the hush of eventide.

Stillness Within

As she walked, surefooted and comfortable in Crea's Crocs, Lyra slowly and intentionally emptied her mind. She let go of all of the new voices of the day, which were repeating powerful messages over and over again, to her once-listening mind. At that time of stillness, when the voices tried again to reenter her quieted center, she let them drift in to her consciousness briefly, and then drift out again, just as quickly. She was instinctively unwinding, and recharging—all in the simple act of coming to inner stillness. This was a coveted state of being.

Lyra recalled the power of the simplest words in Psalm 46 "Be still." She then remembered her favorite sage green ceramic mug for her tea, which was inscribed with those calming words "Be still." She always looked forward to savoring this sentiment, and her tea, in her daily teatime on the veranda. She took these ancient scriptural words to heart, there and then.

She was walking in the last golden rays of the evening, soon to be twilight. *I am walking alone with confidence, knowing fully where I am, and where I am going—simply trusting that all will be well on my journey. No fear. No angst. Simply trusting.*

The colorful aura of peace and contentment that is surrounding me is a perfect summer garden party of Forget-Me-Not-Blue, Pastel Peach, Secret Sage, Champagne Rose, Bella Buttercream Gold, and Lovely Lingering Lavender. Circling around me, is a mystical cloud of stardust—tiny particulate reflectors of light suspended in the sweeping curve of evening light, with me at its center. I can simply feel the beauty of its presence. For a moment, she thought she was imagining the aura, but then, she realized again, that she was tuning in with her spiritual senses.

She walked through the fading evening light, feeling ever so one with Creation, with God—and, peacefully, blissfully, free. She was walking on a pathway of peace, feeling quite at home on a path that was leading her safely, home.

Segue to the Holy Isle

Lyra's mind took an extended segue, to her travels in Scotland last spring. She had traveled to the Western Hebrides, the Islands on the West Coast of Scotland. She had traveled from Glasgow, by train, ferry, bus, and ferry again, to just beyond land's end at the Ross of Mull, to reach her final destination on the tiny Isle of Iona. Her final ferry traversed the windswept Sound of Iona. This very Sound had been the inspiration for many a Scottish lyrical poem, prayer, and song over generations of the original mystical Celtic peoples.

There on Iona, she had attended a retreat. Midway through the retreat, the group of forty pilgrims had trekked around the tiny island on a seven mile adventure over the historic and mystical lands. The Holy Lands of

Scotland. Iona, the Holy Isle. Throughout that daylong rigorous hike, Celtic prayers were offered up, and stories of lore, and tidbits of teachings were shared. The group voiced a collective yearning. They prayed that all peoples everywhere would attune to the Sacred in all life—in all living beings. They prayed that a vision of peace for all peoples, for all lands, would be shared by all.

Christianity was originally brought over to Scotland from Ireland, in the year 563 AD, by Saint Columba, who landed his boat on a southeastern bay of the Isle of Iona, where the powerful ocean forces had created a safe landing space on a beach of smooth rounded rocks and pebbles. In May of last year, Lyra had walked in silence with the large group, one hunderd feet down through a particularly treacherous and steep rocky crevasse, across a boggy plain, and then finally onto the large pebble beach—the shoreline at the head of St. Columba Bay. Accessing this bay was certainly not easy. It was a rugged trek, but worth every physical strain and stress to get there. The pilgrims had all spent their time in deep reflective silence, both in approach to the bay and while exploring the unique bay and shoreline scenery. Lyra recalled, that time there on the stonewashed beach seemed to be suspended. Unhurried. Unrushed. Eternal.

She felt drawn into the antiquity of the place. She wondered then *If only the rocks and stones could speak, and tell of the shoreline stories of yester-year—of how determined the new Irish Christian Monks were to bring their faith and their wisdom to these neighboring shorelines, and to the peoples therein. If only the rocks could tell of their story and trials, of their own needs, and of their precious love of life on the shores.*

Lyra then recalled her sense of being exposed, vulnerable, and present to the elements of nature, yet still so close to God in that shoreline Thin Place. Such a contrast! So close to the edge of the island and the water's edge, yet, so truly centered in her faith and centered in her trust in God! A truly perfect paradox of place and perception!

She had been seriously injured in the Glasgow leg of her journey, having tripped and fallen hard, face first onto the uneven downtown cobblestone sidewalk near the bustling train station. For the rest of her Scottish travels, having to wear a sling on her right arm to support her painful AC joint separation meant her having to slow down quite a bit. She had had to humble herself frequently by asking for help and physical assistance, especially in the treacherous vertical ascent and descent sections of her Iona trek. She had trusted her fellow pilgrims to help her along the way. She'd prayed fervently to God to keep her safe on her journey. She'd known in her heart that one fall was one fall too many for a woman of her age traveling alone in the Scottish wilderness. But she was not truly alone—indeed she had traveled to and from Scotland alone, but she was part of a group full of helpful and caring souls on retreat. And of course, she had known that God was with her. Always.

Lyra recalled that seven-mile pilgrimage on Iona Scotland, to a landmark known as the Hermit's Cell. She could visualize it so clearly. It was at the north end of the island, in the highland, perhaps three hundred feet above the sea level. The nearby rocky coastline was fierce.

Hermit's Cell was a roughly arranged ancient circle of larger rocks, only fifteen feet in diameter, nestled in a hollow grassy basin in a lofty highland elevation. The abruptly rising craggy heights at the edges of the basin created much needed protection from the harsh north and west winds.

When she was in the very center of the Hermit's Cell rock circle, she had noted an absolute absence of sound. No sound of the crashing waves far below. The sound of the wind was totally blocked by the high basin rocky walls. Lyra had lifted up her personal prayers of petition and gratitude while seated in the circle of rocks and surveying the 360-degree, rugged vista. She had felt calm and safe and centered, in this Thin Place at the extreme heights of the northern edge of the island. She knew in her heart that she could trust in God in this harsh yet beautiful setting. Implicit was her trust in God.

It was told that this rock circle in the center of the mountain basin was a favored place for the ancient Christian monks to come to contemplate. Was it possibly a place for the Druidic shepherds to rest in safety and protection from the elements? Some scholars have even questioned the dates and the origins and even the functional significance of the rock circle. Pagan? Norse? Viking? Wiccan even?

Lyra recalled a deep sense of calm and serenity, in this high and protected place. Because of her shoulder injury and having to ask for help, she had humbly extended her trust to all those around her to help her along the way. She couldn't possibly have journeyed alone up to this very special place, this truly Thin Place, with her injury.

Lyra continued striding along in the fading light. After recalling this time of absolute trust, Lyra thought about the ancient well atop the highest height of Iona, just a few hundred paces up the hill from the Hermit's Cell. The elevation was called Dun I. Translated, "the hill of Iona." This was the crowning jewel for Iona. The well itself was said to have been blessed by the Irish Saint Brigid of Kildare, in the fourth century. Lyra recalled words from her retreat classroom notes. "Brigid's blessing was bestowed, that the well waters would carry healing for all those who sought renewal and new beginnings."

Modern day pilgrims were often seen washing their hands or their faces in this legendary well water. Some exuberantly delighted in splashing the water all over themselves. Some, demurely lowered and dipped the tips of their long cloth scarves into the depths of the well and brought the wet scarves up to their faces and necks, for a moment of pure refreshment, renewal, and hope.

Lyra couldn't help but remember one beautiful pilgrim. Julie was an athletic young adult, a seeker in the Celtic Christian faith, on retreat with Lyra. After immersing her face in the waters of the well, while in a yoga handstand, she stood up and slowly lifted her face to the heavens. She smiled and blinked through the moisture on her beautifully water-beaded visage. She had the most blissful and rejuvenated expression on her face. She glowed with an essence of Light from deep within her being.

Lyra had welled up with tears at this sight. Julie was centered there, right at the edge of the well. So precarious in her yoga handstand, yet trusting and safe. So strong in her faith. So confident. Balanced in body, mind and spirit.

Witnessing Julie's moment, Lyra was living vicariously in Julie's exuberant bliss—in Julie's enlivened well-being and her profound trust. Lyra had cried tears of appreciative wonderment. Her tears were full of hope, and gratitude. She then remembered the hug she gave Julie, beside the well. Their hug was a powerful bonding of two souls, two hearts, two Lights—by the still waters—nuanced by eternity, there in the thinnest of all Thin Places.

Oh for the Wings of a Dove

Lyra realized, that as she had been reflecting on her treasured Iona experiences, she had actually crossed through to the outer edge of the deciduous forest and was nearing a meadow, up ahead. The trail would normally guide her around the clearing and straight out to the shoreline of the River Saye.

While she was on the trail, skirting the clearing, she heard the softest cooing of a dove. Sweet. Docile. Gentle. The softness of the coo warmed Lyra's heart. She had a feeling, a feeling of being home, of being welcome.

Then, the impassioned words of Psalm 55 interrupted the coo. Psalm 55 was a prayer of petition spoken by David, the Shepherd, using the winsome image of a dove and its wondrous wings

Oh that I had wings of a dove!
I would fly away and be at rest
Truly I would flee far away
I would lodge in the wilderness
I would find a shelter from the raging wind and tempest.

Lyra sighed in comfort, in the blessed imagery of a dove nestled in the safety of her home in the wilderness.

OPEN YOURSELF TO TRUST

Lyra looked for the source of the gentle cooing sound, and found the sweet mother dove in her nest on a fork of a tree at the very edge of the clearing. She was truly elegant in her royal cloak of muted mocha-mauve-taupe plumage and wispy grey featherings. Lyra made eye contact with the lady dove who repeatedly cocked her head side to side, as if sizing Lyra up. *Perhaps the dove wonders if I am a predator, or not?! Or maybe, just maybe, the tilting of her head is her own macrouran way of beckoning—of welcoming me?*

Before Lyra could entertain any more thoughts on the wonders of this beauty, the dove spoke to her. "Hello Lyra! My name is Aorla! I am a Celtic mystical dove. I'm so glad to see you! You've had a long day and you must be weary from your travels! Come to me, in your weariness. Sojourn with me—rest awhile with me."

Lyra smiled. "Hi Aorla! Thank you! Yes, for sure, I am tired—physically tired. But, I can't help sensing that I'm also energized by my journey today. I've had an emotional dance and a mental feast and a spiritual, mystical pampering today. It's like I've been to an all-day body, mind, and spirit spa. I'm renewed and refreshed. Life is good indeed."

Aorla fluttered her wings for a brief second, while she shifted her position ever so slightly in the nest. "I am nesting right now Lyra. I have two eggs that will hatch in a week or so. You don't mind if I speak to you from up here, do you? I need to keep them warm. My mate, Angus, is out in the wilds, finding food."

A third Angus! Good things always come in threes, Lyra thought. *Angus means "strong." It is good for Aorla, that she has a strong mate! And Aorla means golden. Such a power couple—Golden and Strong! I wonder if she's laid some golden eggs!*

Lyra smiled. As there was no obvious place for her to sit, she leaned against a nearby tree. "Please Aorla, stay where you are. I can hear you and see you very well, from here." Lyra's mind wandered for a millisecond, to her cushioned veranda rocking chair. *My rocker is sooooo comfy!*

Lyra continued. "Let me guess! You have something interesting and important to teach me, but it will require that I open something of mine first, right? So far today, I've been asked to open my eyes, my mind, my heart, and my faith. My curiosity is tickling me. I'm wondering what you will ask of me! Opening my mouth to speak and opening my ears to hear, almost sounds too superficial for such a beautiful dove like you."

Aorla chimed in, "I am a dove, and indeed I am a very symbolic bird. The obvious symbols of peace, love, and hope are known to most religions, cultures, and traditions worldwide. We doves are often believed to be messengers from the Divine, or from the spiritual realm. We are both trusting and trustworthy. We nest at the edges, or the perimeters. We need nearby access to the ground for food and water, but we need to easily get up and away from ground predators. You won't find our nests in the center of the deep woods. With our wider wingspan, that's just too hard to navigate. We prefer vantage points at the edges of forests, meadows and shorelines, up in the first row of trees. For our safety and security, and to help us to be in a position of vigilance, we choose our nesting location carefully. Once we know and trust that we can provide a safe and secure home for our little ones, then we make our babies."

Aorla shifted her position again. "Lyra, your lesson from me is very short, for I know that you embody the core of my lesson already. It is my wish that you carry my message in the forefront of all your conscious living. This will indeed build your strength of character, and empower you for the journey. Trust, will ground and quicken all of your family, social, and Sacred relationships.

"I was very impressed by your Iona reflections as you hiked through the forest. You reflected on the trials of your shoulder injury, where you never once gave up or fell into pieces, saying "Poor me, why me?" You soldiered on with a perseverance that was noteworthy and exemplary. Your trust was unwavering. Despite the severity of your injury and your intense pain while you were on pilgrimage in Iona, you still found the inner strength to muse deeply on ancient locations, ancient people, and ancient wisdom—all of which stirred your heart deeply. You trusted in all of the pilgrims and hosts and Scottish peoples on your journey, that they could and they would lend a helping hand, as your needs emerged and changed. You were one brave woman continuing on your journey with such a mobility-limiting injury. Your steadfastness and perseverance painted a clear portrait of yourself, depicting a woman of faith, whose trust shines like a beacon, who trusts and believes in the essential goodness of humanity, who trusts in God, no matter what.

"And this is my message to you Lyra. Open your trust implicitly, always, no matter what. Open your soul to trust in the Divine—in the Sacred Power—in God—that you will be loved, and secure, and at peace. You need to trust that "your becoming" is a beautiful journey in itself. You need to trust that all will be well in your evolving identity search. Please stay true to all of the teachings of your journey. Trust that you were meant to learn all of these lessons today, here and now, in the moment.

"Your "becoming," your spiritual formation and transformation, and your newfound inner sage soul, will then, synchronously, be bearing fruits at the right time."

Aorla is right. I have already taken a lot of contemplative time over the years, in the name of learning to trust, and in the name of valuing the power and grace of a trusting relationship with God. In her spiritual maturity, Lyra clearly understood the words of Psalm 62, "In God alone I trust. I shall not be shaken."

Lyra already intimately knew through personal experience, about trusting in God. She had faced some hardships in her health long ago, where she had worried relentlessly and needlessly about possible diagnoses and prognoses. It was a time when she didn't place all of her faith and trust in God, who promised to be with her, no matter what. Her learning to trust, was painfully slow.

Lyra had also been in many ER crisis situations at work—cardiac arrests, airway management, dangerous escalating mental health crises, and complicated precipitous births. Situations arose where she never would have managed or conquered without first trusting in her own self—without her intuitive trust in her own sound nursing assessments that a good outcome would prevail in due time. In God's time.

Lyra had faced many family and social relationship struggles over the years, where she simply had to "let go and let God." She had felt she was powerless to steer, or to shape, some very dark and volatile relationships. She'd had to trust that it would all work out well, in the end.

In her Parish Nursing Ministry, Lyra learned to trust her way, to pray her way, to navigate her way, in some very murky healthcare-system waters while advocating for her parish patients' rights and needs. Trusting, and knowing when not to trust, allowed Lyra to rise up with confidence, to lead her patients to the care that they deserved.

And, at age fifty, when it came down to finally getting all of her midlife tattoos done, Lyra had to trust implicitly in her tattoo artists' styles and abilities. They were all tasked with the challenge of creating extensive, watercolor-styled tattoos on Lyra's blank body canvas. Tattoo artists Timea, Joel, and Anthony created one full sleeve, one half sleeve, and a whimsical collage covering her whole back—surreal dreamscapes of images and symbols depicting Lyra's mystical self. And, each one of them rose to the occasion to create their exquisite masterpieces. Lyra was delighted with their artwork, with their beautiful renderings. Lyra knew that her colorful body art was indeed one of a kind. Inked just for her. It gave voice, a certain rhetoric and eloquence, to her own interior life. It detailed the wonders of her life journey. It showcased the colors of her soul. She would never have known this high degree of personal affirmation and validation through this body art, had she not allowed herself to trust in the artists—fully, wholly, completely. In time, Lyra's trust grew.

Lyra smiled, believing that she had been a slow learner regarding trust, but now that she was fully cognizant about needing to trust, she was well on her way on her trust learning curve.

"Yes Aorla, my trust stories of my recent adventures in Iona are solid. And my family, social, and career trust stories are solid as well. Live and learn. Live and learn and grow. Trust in myself. Trust in others. Trust in humanity. Trust in God—always. Trust that all will be well. Trust, is the sturdy footbridge over all troubling waters. Trust, will surely stay and still my soul. Got it!

Off the Beaten Path

Aorla spoke "The sun has set. I need to direct you off the beaten path for the last leg of your journey. The trail ahead is quite boggy after all the rains.

With not much wind to dry it up, it remains totally impassable. Walking through the boggy stuff in your Crocs is not advisable. I'm going to send you across this clearing to the other side, where the path is higher and drier, and you can cut through the woods to the river. You're not far now. I know you're a good navigator, so you shouldn't have any problem finding your way home. Make sure to keep the benevolent Big Dipper squarely behind your shoulders all the time while you're walking. Walk away from the Drinking Gourd, and you will easily get to the path on the River Saye shoreline to home. Got it?"

"Got it, Aorla!" Lyra called out. "Thanks for your kind and clear message, and your directional cues. I am trusting in your directions to get me home safely!"

Aorla offered a gentle farewell coo. Lyra turned and headed across to the far edge of the clearing, onto a new and unknown path to home.

The Word of God
In Real Time—In Prayer

Oh Child of Light,
Blessed are those who trust in God,
whose trust is in God—in me.
They shall be like a tree that is planted by water,
sending out its roots by the stream.
It shall not fear when heat comes,
and its leaves shall stay green.
In the year of the drought, it is not anxious,
and does not cease to bear fruit.
Blessed are those who trust in me.
Blessed are you, My Child of Light. Amen.

At the Altar

Meet Cruith—the Celtic Voice in the Wilderness

Before me stands the Altar of Rock—its Holy Lovelight calls—
Grand rocky outcrop rising through the woodland hallowed halls
In front of me such mystery rides—numinous pure and true
Enlightenment, encouragement, and wonderment ensue.

Lyra's Peniel

Lyra was nearing the rocky shoreline of the River Saye, when she came upon another clearing. In it, she could see an unusual silhouette against the backdrop of moonlit shimmering water and a darkening navy blue sky. It was majestic. Definitely architecturally artistic.

There, a towering presence arose—an asymmetrical mass of granite and dark quartz rocks. Lyra had read about the nurturing powers of the dark blue chalcedony stone that it could absorb negative energy and bring body mind and spirit into peace and harmony. She had been somewhat skeptical in observing these teachings, yet she was open to them, nonetheless.

Might these dark and sparkling rocks be siblings—sisters and brothers—of the mystical chalcedony? Lyra doubted that chalcedony was even mined in Canada, but just the very thought of it was enchanting! *Perhaps the rocks are not even granitic at all! Perhaps they are black obsidian stone—ancient volcanic origin? I wonder if they have a spiritual grounding vibration, if the vibes can heal and bring a grounding harmony. Hmmmmm . . . .*

Lyra had never seen this colossal rock formation before, in any of her woodland travels. But then again, she was presently off the beaten path.

Knowing her whereabouts was *always* important, and indeed, she knew just where she was. Although she was geographically very close to home and physically close to the center of her own familiar world, she did feel quite elated at being *away* from her center and closer to the edge of her understanding, and at the edge of her evolving faith. She was on a new forest path, equipped with her new knowledge, and she was deeply attuning with her spiritual senses—like a child in a mystical leprechaun forest.

She turned her attention to the details of the puzzling pile of rocks. It stretched to possibly forty feet at its center-most height. Its base was as big as a triple car driveway. Lyra felt small beside its massiveness. She was awed to humility by its mystery and in its engineering.

Was it natural? Was it made by human hands? Where did all the granite and dark quartz crystal come from? Was there an historical significance? Was it an ancient royal or religious shrine? Perhaps it was of Indigenous origin? The Anishinaabe? The Ojibwa? The Algonquin? The Cree? Did it have a directional function like a northern Inuit Inukshuk, or an Algonquin Waypoint?

Perhaps it isn't even ancient at all. What if it is a contemporary Canadian artist's abstract rendering—a one of a kind woodland wilderness sculpture, with a symbolic message to the world? If that is the case, I am sure I would have known about the existence of such a striking sculpture, through my community! But, I don't.

Looking again at the Great Rock Altar, not only did the rocks and crystals reflect the light of the moon, but they had a luminous quality all of their own. They glowed. A silvery lavender shimmery Light emanated, as if from a source from within. *A Theophany? A Shining? A Shimmering?*

Lyra then recalled Old Testament Jacob's rock altar. Jacob created a rock monument at the riverside, at the place where he wrestled in the night with God in his dream. In the Genesis account of the story, the name of that riverside memorial, was Peniel, which was translated from Hebrew to mean "face-to-face with God." *Is this Altar of Rock and Light, here in the Buchanan Lakes District, truly a modern day Peniel? Am I dreaming? Am I, Lyra, about to come face-to-face with God? Hmmmmm . . . .*

A Voice in the Wilderness

Oddly, she thought she heard someone call her name. She looked directly at the Altar of Rock and Light, looking for the speaker. Seeing no one, she called out "Hello? Is someone there? Did someone call my name?"

An easy going, androgynous voice answered "Hi Lyra. I am Cruith! Nice to see you out here in this neck of the woods!"

"Hello Cruith! I cannot quite make out your form. Where are you? Can you please step forward so I can see you?"

"Hey Lyra, I have no form. I'm kind of laid back—I'm here, but I'm not. I am a mystical Celtic Voice in the wilderness. I live here in the forest, in the timelessness of natural rock and Light. My voice carries with it the tremor of truths, the vibes of vitality, and the very emanance of energy. My voice channels streams of creativity, artistry, and uniqueness like a river running through all time—like a flood of Light from a Higher, Greater Source. Sort of like a vibrant vocal version of your Holy Lovelight!

"You will hear my vocal tones clearly in your own language, in your very deepest depths. I am probably your last waypoint of the day. The sun has now set. Twilight is here and the moon is high in the sky. You'll be heading home from here, very soon."

"Cruith, oh my goodness! I'm afraid you've taken me by surprise! I've been talking to so many unique living creatures today! They are my new-found forest friends! They are all mystical beings. They all have taught me some important life lessons. But it seems you are different in your physical-ity—a rather uncreaturely being! You have such a grand physical presence here in the moonlit clearing, yet, you still give the ambiance of ease—of friendliness, openness, and welcome.

"If you had eyes, I know for sure that we would be feeling strongly connected in making constant eye contact with each other. Your voice is warm and encouraging. I feel strangely and incredibly drawn into your presence, here by the shining waters of the Saye. I feel nurtured and cared for. I feel gathered in by your grace. Cruith, I am totally at peace here, with you."

Lyra stepped a little closer into the Grand Altar's impressive, yet com-fortable space. She was becoming aware of a sweet juxtaposition—a sharp contrast in her spatial awareness. There, in that very moment, she felt an unexpected centering. She actually felt cozy, as though she was nestled and all curled up in a veranda chair—as if she were sitting prayerfully, in God's lap. She had a sense of being close to her own comfort zone—and closer still, to her own beliefs. She felt grounded there, centered, at home—all the while standing at an unfamiliar altar—while being at the edge of her understanding. Talk about a paradox, or perception *abuptio*, or a Tsunami-sized paradigm shift!

She reached toward the back of her head and released all of her curls, automatically returning the scrunchie in readiness, to its home around her right wrist. She tossed her head, gently, side to side, allowing her snow-white curls to cascade down, to tumble freely into their own place of comfort—to settle in where they would. *I am comfortable. I feel free. Symbolically unleashed, unbridled, I am me. I'm present. I'm open. I'm real.*

Lyra sighed. She was just then noticing she was both physically tired and mentally weary, from her lengthy conversations of the day. But, she was alive with curiosity for the perfect-English-speaking voice of the Altar of Rock and Light. "Cruith, I'm looking forward to your message. If you are as you say, my last waypoint of the day, then your message must be the best. Like they all say, the best for the last!"

She continued "I am close to home. Just down there at the shoreline, I'll turn left and follow the river just a short piece, to my home."

Cruith spoke again. "Yup, you are close to home at this late hour, but before you get there, I've got a lesson—more like some coaching—for you Lyra. I know you're tired, but I also know that you—especially you—will 'get me, and get my words'. For you Lyra, are the creative one. Yours is the Creative Life."

And they went on "You are a poet, and a composer, and a wannabe musician. Your gardens are full of color and texture. Your woodland natur-escapes rock! Your original recipes—Pears Olivia, and Hickory Haystack Eggs, and Brussel Bites—are delish! Your crafts and quilts are one of a kind. Your church liturgical works are moving and meaningful. Your original Sunday School plays are hilarious! Who could ever forget "Little Revi's Dream," or the dramedy "She Didn't Say Amen"? Your creativity shines in everything you do! You have an awesome green thumb in the creative world!"

Cruith paused and shifted gears. "Lyra, you already know how to think outside the box. I need to teach you *more* than that. It's about boundaries. Creative boundaries—your perceived obstacles and boundaries in your own creative realm. Is it okay if I talk about this a bit, before I give you your sixth spiel of the day?"

"Please Cruith! I am truly the privileged one, to glean any pearls of wisdom from you, and from all of my new forest friends. You have all given me waypoints of wisdom, and mystical checkpoints in truth and reality, and in time. I have been holistically pampered all day long, reaching over thresholds into new mindsets and into mystery.

Cruith was an articulate genius in their *laissez-faire* world of creativity. Their vocal presence and affect was that of both magnetic mentor, and cool go-to artist-in-residence.

In the sublimity of the current moment, Cruith was simply an ethereal voice that Lyra was drawn to listen to. She needed to discern their relevance in her life—in her artistry—and in her whole creative realm.

OPEN YOURSELF TO THE LIGHT

Cruith opened by saying "Creativity is a gift. Creativity knows no boundaries. My simple lesson is this, Lyra. Open up your creative boundaries! Open yourself to the wideness and the wildness of creative expression! Open yourself to the Light!

"Lose all of your boundaries when entering into your creative realm. Express yourself with reckless abandon. Step past all boundaries, walls, and norms. Break out your wild!

"Be a dreamer. The world needs dreamers. Dream when you're awake. Personify the inanimate. Imagine living without limits. Unbridle your inner child's play. Believe in yourself and in your gifts. Believe that you can, and you will."

Lyra nodded. She was loving Cruith's train of thought. She was taking it all in.

Cruith went on "Open up to your inner creative Light! You were given the gift of creativity with good reason. Explore your creative realm. Find the dark side. Expose the Light side. See the fringe areas and the grey zones. Show the rough and raw edges.

"Find the seductive draw. Let suggestive heats arise from your medium. Build unexpected tensions there. Put tension out there, between the lines, or between the music notes, or between the images. In canvas, lyrics, music, or pure fiction, make your art ask questions, not answer them!"

Lyra was on fire with renewed creative energy. She resolved to include Cruith's concepts in her upcoming writing endeavors. She vowed to evolve her style, her artistry, her boundaries.

"Cruith, you are speaking generally, because you are speaking of creativity in all media. Maybe you could tell me more about the art of creative writing. I've been writing poetry and liturgies and song lyrics for a long time now. I love words! I love morphing words—portmanteauing in prosetry. I love creating characters and making them come alive! I love writing, and unscrambling ideas until truth and new Light emerge. My works have always been designed to quicken the mind, energize the body, and awaken the soul. Any thoughts on where to go next with my writing? I'm all ears! And what did you mean when you said 'Open yourself to the Light?' That sounds kind of 'out there!'"

Cruith continued on, with greater passion and purpose, appealing to Lyra's receptive heart. "In your chosen medium, tell a story. Tell *your* story. Teach a lesson. Write a book. Shift into fiction. Show off your imagination and originality. Look past the walls of religion, politics, sociology, and biology. And truly see your story. Present your story, twist your storyline—and its ending.

"Make your readers want to be a part of your story. Make them want to experience with you, all of the highs and lows. Through your experiential story and your lessons-between-the-lines, make them want to know you and care for you. Make them fall in love with your characters. When you laugh, they'll laugh. When you cry, they'll cry with you. When you birth a new work of art or a novel, they'll want to share in your journey and share in your joy. They'll live vicariously in your art, and in your works."

Lyra's eyes were wide. She quivered in her excitement. She was inspired. Cruith was a goldmine. Cruith was a guru of artistic expression. Cruith was dictionary for creativity.

Oh my! The omnivolent and androgynous Cruith is giving me permission to move forward, to create in a boundary-free headspace. They're giving me a tabula rasa! I'm desperately wishing that I had my notebook and pencil with me. I hope that down the road, I can have Cruith as my mentor!

Lyra already knew a lot of these creativity terms and tricks of the trade. In her heart of hearts, she also knew that a true artist uses all of these techniques seamlessly, with refined flare and finesse. *The true artist delights in using sweet elements of surprise, and, in the je ne sais quoi. The artsy it-factor is truly reverenced by all artists, in all media.*

Lyra extrapolated Cruith's words, and concluded, *The finished art canvas or novel or full music score, has the inherent power to beckon, befriend, and embolden. It can cry out—scream—with passion. A wee dash of daring and a splash of swagger can lurk between the lyrical lines—even within the cadence of the soulful melody. Creativity can crest beneath the artist's clever hand.*

Cruith still had more to share. "Open your creative boundaries, Lyra! Open yourself to the Light! Allow the Light to flow through you. It will, in return, open you to so much more—more color, more depth, more insight, more perspective, more truth, more Light. Simply, more. The Light is within you—it is yours—find it—feel it—let it lead you—let it shape and shade you. Light into Light.

"Do this now, and pour your whole self into your creativity. You have the time. You have the gift. You will come up for air one day, and you'll understand first hand, the meaning of creativity without boundaries. And, your new works—your outside-the-box works—will reflect this. Your expressions will be Light. You, Lyra, are Light."

The Warmth and the Glow

Deep in thought, Lyra reached out to touch the Altar. She picked up a small shimmering rock and clasped it by her heart. And to her delight, she felt an incredible warming flow running into her hands from the Altar rock, up through her arms, and then throughout her whole body.

Did I just receive a creative energy transfer, by merely touching the Altar of Rock and Light? Was this another Holy Moment, or a Thin Place in the Presence of the Divine? Was this an epiphany? Am I forever changed in this moment? Transformed? Transcending? Did I just become something more than myself?

Wow! In my wide wide-openness, I am energized, alive, and ready. Ready for what, I do not know. The term "divine spark" comes to mind. This is such a formative place and time. Hmmmmm . . . .

Lyra began to speak to Cruith, and then stopped suddenly, when she noticed that the Light in the Altar had gone dim, and the rocks were notably cool. She stepped back, and sat down beside the Altar and silently prayed.

God, there is so much that I just do not understand. But you have perpetually been by my side, encouraging me, as I journeyed today. This was a nature walk to remember, for sure! How can I thank you enough for this gift of your Presence, your Ever-Presence, and for your amazing plans for my life? I'm honored. I'm humbled. With a grateful heart, I say thank you!

Her gratitude continued to pour out. *"Thank you" just isn't big enough of a phrase to express all of the gratitude in my heart. May I be and may I become that humble soul which will please you. May I serve you well, using all of the blessings and the gifts you have given to me. My Kindest Shepherd, and My Gentle Pastor, please hear my heart—please hear my prayer. Amen.*

Shine!

Lyra felt something. She closed her eyes, remaining seated. When she noticed a sense of wonderment suffusing her, she smiled. This was yet another moment of spiritual awakening. Another moment of attuning with her spiritual senses. Another moment of feeling an indescribable beauty all around her and within her. She lay back on the ground, her curly locks sprawling out all around her. She held onto Cruith, close to her heart.

Lyra opened her eyes and looked straight up at the stars. *So much twinkling and Light in the darkness! So much delight to simply be—in Mystery—underneath a shimmery, sparkly scene, a starry starry celestial sea! An awesome Symphony of Light, in the Grand Concert Hall of the Heavens—of Life.*

She felt a pulsating energy within. A thrill. A rush. A natural high. A subtle flow and warming burst of the Holy Lovelight from within her heart. *What a day! Such a journey from the center of the world I know, to the edges of the unknowns and back again. Best nature walk ever!*

As she lengthened her focus, she gazed beyond the stars, beyond the galaxies. And, way beyond the heavens, she saw it. It was iridescent and colorful, like the veil from earlier in the day. But, it was moving, forming and unforming in a nebulous flow, like the Aurora Borealis. It had an energy, a Sacred presence. Her mind wandered and she created the words—*Fractalificent, and Kaleidurreal.* Then she mused, *Metaform meets Metamystique. Metapresence meets Metanow.*

She sighed. For a few sweet moments, her mind drifted. Lyra drifted. Oblivion nestled in. Contentment settled in.

The energy source that she was watching, was light-years away, yet it graced her inner being. Lyra knew she was in a liminal space. A time of transcendence. A moment of grace that called to her soul.

And then she heard it—a voice traversing all time and space. God spoke to her once again. "My Beloved. My Child. You are mine. Shine brightly like the stars. Shine brightly from within. Simply, shine." For Lyra, the clearest bidding of all was God's last word, "Shine!"

Lyra literally, saw the Light, then and there. Lyra understood her pathway. She could see the way forward. *This is my moment. This is my time—my time to shine brightly! Through Cruith, I can see the truth. I have the knowledge. I have the gift. I have the interest and the creative spark. And God is calling me to shine brightly. All I need is conviction. Confidence too. I have all the encouragement in the world, in Cruith. I just need to turn inward, and look into my depths—look for the Light deep within me. I need to allow the Light to flow through me, to course through me, to surge like a tsunami, bursting over any of my preconceived boundaries, or limitations, or barriers. I need to let the Light lead me. I need to live in the Light.*

She felt a mental head rush in a sudden flight of ideas. Her mind was alive. The Creative Life was calling her—loudly. It was time for her to write, with the intent of publishing, with the intent of sharing her gift. It was time for her to teach the tenets of the ancient Celtic Wisdom to a broader audience, a literary audience. It was time for Lyra's words to be known, loved, and understood. It was time for her words to shine.

Best-Forest-Friends-Forever Reunite

Lyra stood up. The moonlight danced across the waters. She walked toward the sparkling Light. The Saye was only paces away.

"May we join you, Lyra?"

Lyra startled. Another unexpected voice! "Who's there?" she called out.

"Turn around Lyra. We're all here with you. We're here to get you safely home. You must be tired after your illuminating journey!"

Lyra turned and looked all around herself in the clearing by the shore. To her amazement, she found that she was encircled by all of her newfound friends of the forest. "Zoli! Yala! Xavad! Aorla! A small chunk of Cruith was still held firmly in her left hand. "Where's Bradn?"

"He comes and goes quickly" said Yala "He needs water. He'll mystically appear and disappear as he needs to. Look! There he is now!"

Lyra broke into a great big smile. Bradn had just then, leaped out of the river and was soaring in midair, right in front of her. She quickly reached out, and his sparkly body landed with a loud smacking sound, safely in her outstretched forearms. A single iridescent bubble blossomed, and burst over his glistening gills. Their eyes met, and for a precious moment, they shared a tender greeting.

Lyra embraced Bradn and all of his wisdom. She held both him and Cruith close to her heart. All seven Celtic souls bonded, as a comforting cloak of interconnectedness covered over them.

They all began to walk on the trail, together, instinctively towards the River Saye—the magnificent River Saye which they all knew and loved—which they all called home.

A motley crew they were, for sure—some kindred spirits and sweet sage souls, and best forest friends forever—BFFF's! They were united in mystical energy. They were an awesome assembly of ancient Celtic symbolic wildlife. They were plugged in, tuned in, and exquisitely aware of the Holiness within each other—and of the Sacred space wherein they journeyed. They all, deep in their hearts, felt the draw of home—the centering call of home.

At the very moment when Lyra and her gang arrived at the moonlit sparkling waters, Bradn leaped out of Lyra's arms into the river. He swam around, accelerating in a few fast circles, and then leaped again into Lyra's arms. Water was so important to him. Right there at the shore of the River Saye, Lyra stopped and addressed her friends. "My dear friends, I feel like I've known all you forever. I feel comfortable here with you. We have experienced a great deal together today.

My heart is light with joy, laced with love and gratitude,
my words a-tumbling-frenzy now, from deep within to you.
For God has been here with me, walking with me—with us all.
Most surely present to us, all the day and evening long.

And it is time to acknowledge

the gift of God's Presence
and the gift of our own awareness
and the gift of the blessedness in Lovelight iridescence.

Can we do that? Can we join together in prayer, here by the

fresh flowing waters
and the calm running waves
of the Great River Saye
in the great riverscape that we all call home?"

The forest friends came into stillness together, and Lyra spoke out her endearing prayerful words, in one truly Holy Moment at the Great Rivershore:

"God of all Creation
You are here.
You are Sacred.
You are Mystery.
You are Light.
You are rock and tree and sky and sea.
We don't see you—
but, we do.
We cannot touch You, but, we are touched by You.
We know You—
in the wildness, in the warmth, in the wind.
We reverence You—
at the Thin Place—at the center—and at the farthest edge.
And, as this day dwindles into the depths, and into the dark of night,
we call out to You,
in humility, and in hope, and in gratitude.
Your deep peace graces our hearts, and quiets our souls.
We settle and rest in Your love.
Like the quiet, constant, peaceful running wave onto the shores,
You are Eternal.
You are here with us. Thanks be. Amen."

The Word of God
In Real Time—In Prayer

Oh Child of Light,
Arise and work, create,
and I will be with you.
Arise, shine, for your Light has come,
and my glory is rising within you.
Be strong in the Light, My Child. Amen.

Toward Sabbath

Meet Zaba—The Celtic Sound of the Eternal

I turn for home, the river so deep, three muses in my head—
Enlivened by my journey now—grounded, grateful in debt.
Sojourning free in comfort and peace—to rest, to breathe, renew—
My Sabbath in the Center? Edge?—to contemplate, to muse.

Peculiar Parade

Zoli, Yala, Bradn, Xavad, Aorla, and Lyra all lifted up their eyes after they shared in prayer at the shore. Cruith simply envisioned the heartwarming moment. By the still waters, the group members made eye contact, one by one, and smiled inwardly. They were newly bonded in friendship, and in the sharing of wisdom, and just then, through the power of prayer. How delighted they were to be together, for they all had communed in their own special way on Lyra's wonderful inland—and inward—journey.

Where they had emerged from the forest, at the river shore, was about one hundred yards north of Lyra's property line. They laughed and sang and pranced and darted about, knowing that they now had time to play and to relax, all of them, together.

Then the real fun began. The impromptu royal pageantry and parade of forest sages, benevolent celestial souls, and friends of the deep, followed the edge of the forest at the rocky shoreline. They threw their cares to the wind. For any onlookers, their dark silhouettes against the brightly moonlit shores would have been such a sight to behold! But, there were no onlookers—no witnesses—no one to verify or to embellish this story of their frivolity and lighthearted fun. They all paraded on the path in single file, processional style, sporting their creaturely crowns and their colorful regalia.

Some were flitting or fluttering, or kicking up their hooves. Some were soaring and swooping, or warbling and woohooing. Xavad actually pranced for a few carefree steps! His giant teeth shone bright in the night as he grinned with joy. Then he marched, standing up tall on his two hind legs, with his stately rack of antlers reaching up on high, to the sky. Xavad was becoming exceedingly bold and relentless, in loudly banging his front hooves together, high up out in front of him. Like clinking clunking cymbals. He was not subtle, or unassuming, in his leading of the parade—in keeping the rhythm for all at the end of the day.

Yala, the silken black raven, landed on Lyra's head. She performed, swaying in a two-step dance. She followed with a lively Irish jiglike number. Her fancy feathered physique stayed perfectly erect, while she used her quick and intricate footwork to tread with finest precision amongst Lyra's tangled mop of frizz and curls. Lyra couldn't actually see Yala up on the top of her head, but her head could feel every magical, mystical step of the dance. Yala's long tail feathers trailed in Lyra's longer lengths of softly cascading curls, seemingly becoming "one-with."

And Zoli, at one point, alighted high up on Lyra's chest, on her left collarbone. Zoli simply remained there, ever so still, all the while ablaze with a grand showing of her sparkling Light. Zoli's Light was billowing, much like the fluid Northern Lights up high in the starry sky. Her compound eyes were glittering, like the spinning silver disco balls of yesteryear. There was a resounding peacefulness in that time and space. Zoli's presence intimated Sacredness—her Light waxed mystical—the moment was truly timeless. Time stood still.

Aorla flapped her wings rhythmically with Xavad's beat, and she crooned and cooed in her own happy tune. And, Cruith—with one voice or three?—was chanting so free in sweet harmony—with voices aloft in the rocks and the trees. *Hmmmmm . . . . And I, for real, I can hear, I can feel, all the sounds and the songs of grand cacophony!*

Bradn's gills needed to be wet, and he leaped again into the shallow waters. He stayed there, precision swimming in figure eights, gracefully. His scales shimmered in the moonlight, regal and resplendent in the waters of the Saye.

All were exuberant in their shared joy of being. Such a peculiar vignette out of the most eclectic dreamscape! Such joie de vivre in unrehearsed pomp and circumstance! So much togetherness—in the starlight—in the Lovelight.

The whimsical parade and play, then totally evolved. It morphed and took on a scene of solemn serenity.

As if on cue, all noise and songs simply ceased and silence entered their souls. An unmistakable calm swept in and moored in their midst. Mystery mantled the milieu.

Reverently, in a rhythmical dance, the gathered friends entered the shallows of the moving waters. Their steps quiet, slow and sure—their souls intrepid. Billowing Light surrounded each one, and floated—flowed—angelically behind and before them as they moved. An ineffable sight. Lyra was touched. She merged her words inwardly. *This is Lovelightesque, Metascopic, Adulariant.*

They traveled downstream, with the current. The only audible sound was the waters of the River Saye lapping gently on the shore. Their Light was translucent and soft. Luminous veil-like wisps trailed from their arms and legs, antlers, wings and gills. Feathers in the Lovelight lifted aloft in transcendence on the Holy Breath, above the fervor of the flowing *fleuve.* Lyra's cascading curling tresses glistened in the moonlight, gracing her, etherealizing her, crowning her wholesome presence. Illumination was arising from a source deep within each one of them. A certain aura of peacefulness, blanketed over them in their nebulous, yet clarifying Light.

Then, at the right time, they returned to their frivolity. They all joined in a traditional circle dance. A stirring celebratory step-dance. Hands and hooves and rocks were held. Fish frolicked in the river. The winged ones alighted on her shoulders and on her head. Lyra circle-danced in the waters of the smooth rock shoreline right in front of her home with all her new acquaintances, all at once.

Dazzling Lovelight is flowing and glowing, and besparkling within and through each and every one of us! Such unity, joy and spontaneity. Such an overwhelming sense of being part of something truly greater than our single selves—an overwhelming sense of belonging. Such oneness!

This scene of ebullient wonderment was about to be further enriched by an exquisitely engaging sound. The Voice—the Sound of the Eternal.

Alpha and Omega Bookends

A gentle voice from out of nowhere and everywhere addressed Lyra, calling her by her name. "Hello Lyra, it's Zaba speaking. I am here for you. I am with you. I am only an ethereal voice in time. You cannot see me, but I know you can hear me, because you have listened to me all of your life. You may feel the warmth and the comfort of my presence—you may even feel the wonder of my presence. You might experience the Light of my formless being through my calling and through my voice—even throughout Creation in the joy of my songs of life—everywhere-present in the music of the spheres.

"Psalm 139 is a string of beautiful passages, describing the Holy Everpresence in your life. Revelations 21:6 does this as well. 'I am the beginning and the end. The Alpha and the Omega.' I am truly like all of your creaturely messengers today. The first letters of all of our names, are from the very beginning of the alphabet, or, from the very end of the alphabet. We are like bookends. We are all so symbolically embracing your formation and your becoming, from the beginning to the end. We are symbolically surrounding you, and teaching you. We are encouraging you, and challenging you from start to finish. We are symbolically with you, always.

The Journey

"You, Lyra, have had one extraordinary, experiential day. You have been graced by the Holy Lovelight throughout your woodland journey. You have witnessed the wonders of God's Creation, by the shores of the great River Saye, and you've delighted in the magnitude of its inherent sage wisdom. You have moved away from having a fire in your head to having a Light in your very being. Your essence—your Lovelight—is shining brightly. You, Lyra, are shining brightly!

"You have waded in and wandered through many important life-lessons today. You have accepted the elements of mystery and mystique. You graciously allowed mythology and mysticism to simply be—you embraced

Holy Mystery with a wide-open heart, mind, and spirit. You have learned, discerned and grown as you willfully opened yourself to receive.

"Your spiritual formation journey is truly ongoing, calling you to become most fully human. Your becoming, is your lifeblood. Your becoming, is your pathway. Your becoming, is your channel and your connection to your God. Your becoming, is truly your grace. In the coming days and weeks you will see your becoming, in a whole new perspective, in a whole new frame, in a whole new Light."

Lyra remained still and attentive. Open and receptive. She loved listening to Zaba's summation of her centered, sage and Sacred self. She felt intensely drawn to Zaba, with a connection that was beyond any utterable notion. She was interconnected in the cosmos—in the matrix and the web, in the fractals and the spirals—in the life-breath of all life and living.

Lyra—at the shore of the River Saye, just steps away from her riverside home, surrounded by the wisdom of the ages and the wisdom of the sages, her new forest friends, in the presence of the ethereal voice, Zaba—was content. She was whole. She was One. She was blessed—she was blissed—in body, mind and spirit.

OPEN YOURSELF TO GOD

Zaba spoke assertively "My one and only lesson for you comes from Genesis, in the beginning of the Bible. And my Alpha and Omega words are from Revelations, at the last of the Bible. I hope that these bookend Scriptures and all of the imbedded scriptural references made today will rest easy on your heart, and that they will work through you as only Light can do."

And Zaba continued. "It is as simple as this. You need to rest in God. Open yourself to the Sacred, to the Holy, to God. Open yourself to reverence, to worship, to Sabbath. Open yourself—intimately and fully—to God.

"You have truly labored your mind all day, learning and applying and embodying six amazing life lessons. In opening your eyes, mind, heart, faith, trust, and creativity, you have birthed a whole new you! Your work is done! Your newest Spiritual Formation Story is now complete!

"Your seventh lesson is about resting from your diligent work. God did wonderful works in six days, and on the seventh, he rested. You are a faithful, religious woman, spiritually emanating and intimately connected to the Eternal, by the River, and by the Light deep within.

"Please take time now to rest with your God, and to rest your soul. Find renewal and peace in your Sabbath rest. Rest with God. Rest in God. Rest in the Sacred."

A Different Spin

Lyra lifted her face as if to address her comments to some physical being directly in front of her. She spoke facing forward, although she knew not from where the friendly disembodied voice came. It was a unique and profound surround sound experience, to say the least.

"Zaba," she said slowly "I am ready to rest my body, mind and spirit, for sure. I need that kind of Holy rest—that wholesome healing rest—deep down in my soul.

"But Zaba, I do have a gnawing restlessness, and I think I know where it is coming from. I have previously wrestled with the psychology term, 'cognitive dissonance.' Simply put, it is the common human state of having inconsistent thoughts, beliefs, or attitudes, especially related to behavioral decisions or attitude change. Like saying one thing and doing another, or, believing one thing, but living in the complete opposite actions to that belief.

"And, I also know about the term 'egocentricity.' That is where an individual is, or becomes, totally focused on themselves, their thoughts and their beliefs—they become the center of their own lives. In my own life, I do consciously and consistently try to say and do the same thing. I'd be a common hypocrite if I didn't! And I do really try to keep an open and worldly perspective, such that I *am not* the center of my whole life.

"But," she continued, "after all of my lessons today that are directed inwardly toward me, myself, my person, my being—me me me—my my my—this all sounds so painfully egocentric and therefore extremely cognitively dissonant for me. Here, I profess to be a loving, compassionate woman, choosing to serve others, but my lessons are teaching me to focus on myself, to understand the very core of me, in the name of becoming the best version of me—Lyra 2.0. I'm really not resisting the content of my new lessons, but I do think I am beginning to struggle all over again, with all of this me-focus, and what seems to me to be self-centered egocentricity."

Lyra continued, "I also have a strong negative internal gut reaction to the modern phrase 'It's all about me.' Folks use it all the time to describe the seeming superficial, ego-centered, and sometimes narcissistic people in their midst. I find all of the shallow behaviors, hollow emotions, and the driven self-importance to be detestable, disgraceful, and I admit from a purely judgmental perspective—shameful.

"I would hope that folks would never, ever, view me like that. With my newly spiritually formed version of me, I would hope that I would never be misread, or misperceived as an ego-centered mess. I feel, and I want others to recognize, that my interior work is not selfish, nor self-serving—rather, it is Holy, Sacred, Blessed—that my interior work leads me on a lifelong path towards becoming most fully human. And I do feel quite comfortable in all of these holistic and formative words. Most importantly, I need to feel genuinely comfortable, on my pathway to becoming most fully human."

Zaba allowed a cloud of silence to hover. Zaba then spoke these words of encouragement "Lyra, you know your psychology and behavior theories well. So it should not be hard for you to put the right spin on all of this. You need to be comfortable, not struggling, on your own identity-seeking journey. Let me help you gain a more insightful perspective.

"You do know the process of knowing the self is called 'interior work,' and that no one can do this but you. Once you do your homework in opening yourself to becoming most fully human, then you will be equipped to do the work you are being called to do.

"Think of your interior work as your own personal in-service-training. It is just one of many small workshops in a lifetime commitment of continuing education, and a lifetime of becoming. This *is not* egocentricity, *nor* is it self-centered. It *is* inward focused interior work in the name of acknowledging your true self as God's Beloved—God's Child of Light—in the fullest sense of the terms.

"You are on a lifelong journey of learning and spiritual formation. You are an integrity-based, faith-based person, living the Christlike life, offering peace and love and hope to people, and to the world. You have lived in the Compassionate Life, serving others with your servant heart. You are equipping yourself, so that you can help others. You are using your God-given gifts to serve others. Does that create a better perspective, for you Lyra?"

"Zaba, Oh my! Thank You! You are wise. So very wise. I can really see what you mean, when you put it in such simple terms. Your use of the in-service analogy makes your lesson so relevant. You are an amazing teacher. That was a perfect parable-like image, from which I can learn.

"And, hey Zaba! I don't feel that restless sensation anymore—I do want to feel peace, and contentment. I do want to feel centered, and at home with me. As a matter of fact, I am just starting now, in this very moment, to begin to feel a warmth and peacefulness in the calmness of your healing words and encouraging voice." Her voice trailed off. "I am weary."

Namaste

Zaba reiterated "Are you ready now to find renewal and peace in your Sabbath? Are you ready to open yourself to God?" Zaba paused, "Are you ready to rest in God?"

Lyra nodded in affirmation. She turned back toward her circle of newfound friends. They had been listening attentively to Zaba's wisdom. They were all fresh new acquaintances and, at once, soul friends—Anam Cara of the Deep. Theirs was a beautiful bond, both in Lyra's being and in her becoming. Their mentoring would most surely shape and season the breath and the breadth of Lyra's evolving identity.

Lyra bent down and gently placed Cruith in the water, feeling the thud as they landed on the river rock floor. "I'll never forget you my friend. Never ever! You are an inspiration. My artful mentor. You have shined your Light of creative genius into the depths of my very being. Thank you." Bradn drifted in the waters, beside Cruith, right in front of Lyra.

Lyra stood up slowly, gracefully. She gave a heartfelt silent namaste bow to each of her friends, one by one. Her own heart softly spoke these words with each bow: *The Sacred in me, bows in reverence, to the Sacred in you.* And they too nodded and bowed to Lyra, in honor and in deepest respect. Then, as if on command, they willingly scattered away to their own homes in Creation. They swam and walked and winged their way home— all of them—in the waters, in the wind—in the wonder of the wilds—in the truth of all time—in the tangents and the tangles of true timelessness. Lyra's little court of Celtic mystical beings, her motley crew of compelling companions, parted in company only, for their hearts would remain ever-connected, interconnected. Their hearts would be linked for life. Linked in love, linked by their Sacred Light within.

Lyra stood in the river, and watched them all disperse to begin their own journeys home. She lifted her eyes heavenward and gazed into the spellbinding starshine. She knew instinctively for what she was searching. She easily located the constellation Lyra—her namesake constellation—directly overhead in the nearing-midnight-sky. She felt one, contented, understood, identified. Lyra was whole.

Lyra lingered long in the mystery of the moment, in the twinkling of the twilight. Then she raised hers arms overhead, palms facing upward to the heavenly dome, as if she was engaging in full-on prayersong. She slowly pulled both hands, clasped together, to her heart, and she bowed forward with gratitude, to the everywhere-present Zaba. The timeless and omnipresent Zaba embraced her—with silence—with Presence—with love. The voice of the Eternal had spoken.

Lyra had finally arrived at the shores of her home, very late in the evening. *Home at last! My own home sweet home by the river. I guess it's approaching the midnight hour. The brilliant moon is beautiful, and high in the sky. There is so much Light. It is still Saturday. Sabbath is near.*

The Word of God
In Real Time—In Prayer

My Blessed Child,
Sabbath follows six days of labor,
six days of work and toil.
Your six lessons today were laborious and heavy,
mentally and emotionally draining.
Come to me in your weariness.
Come to me in your fatigue.
Rest in me, rest in your Sabbath.
Rest and commune with me.
Rest, take time to be Holy.
I will satisfy you, and replenish you, My Blessed Child. Amen.

Home—By the River
Lyra

Beyond the River beckons the Light with mystical allure—
It draws my curiosity—I come intrigued for sure.
May I be opened to its sweet call—in body, mind and soul
May I be changed, transformed—transcending—Becoming truly whole.

Home Sweet Home

Lyra emerged from the river shallows, yet seemingly from the depths. With her every step over the flat rocks, her feet squeaked noisily, soggy inside Crea's Crocs.

Lyra approached her home, up the path from the river, up the two steps, onto the screened-in veranda, and over to the rocker on the brook-side. She stepped out of the very loud lime-green shoes that had literally saved the day. She flopped herself gratefully into the deep comfy chair, and she tucked her heels up underneath her. She was pulling a sun-faded quilt over her legs, when Paidi came into the room. Looking a little sleepy-eyed, she asked to be picked up. Lyra reached out and brought Paidi up to her face. Little love-licks abounded. Paidi squirmed for only a moment, and then settled. It was well past her bedtime. *Do I ever have a story to tell you, my sweet Paidi-pie—someday. Hmmmmm . . . .*

Lyra let her own thoughts run free. A colorful 3D HD vignette graced her field of vision. She saw herself in the vision, cross-legged in her oversized hanging basket chair in the grand oak tree grove of her woodland garden, under a peachy-pastel sunset sky. Mist courted the river. Her long white cascading curls sparkled in the horizontal light, framing her visage. Her countenance of perfect peace glowed. Her whole person simply sparkled in the wonder of the Holy Lovelight. She was holding a luminous golden lyre—an ancient Celtic harp. She was softly strumming the instrument while gazing out over the smooth rock shores of the River Saye, opening up into the Baye of Saye. There were no echoes. There were no symphonies, or angel choruses. Just the exquisite soulful pleasure of Lyra's lyre. Chipmunks and bunnies and birds all were still, mesmerized by her song and her words. Cicadas, crickets and frogs were silent. Lyra let that idyllic vision, simply fade in her mind.

Then, she took up her notebook and pencil. She was only going to write down fragments of images, and descriptive phrases, and maybe a few buzzwords, lest she forget the important details and the sequences of her daylong odyssey.

She mentally summarized her Sacred Learning from the day. And she spoke these words softly, inwardly, with heartfelt conviction. *I am shining! I am shining brightly!* She finally felt completely comfortable in saying these stirring words. She spoke to herself again, this time her inner voice was a little louder. In her very confident interior voice: *I, am becoming. All life is Sacred. I am Sacred. My words are Sacred. My life is Sacred.* And with an even more dramatic tone, of deep gratitude, she enunciated her glowing, impassioned praise. *God is with me. Thanks be to God. Amen.*

Let my story unfold. Let my affirmations be heard. Let my story arise. Let my story become. I am responding to God's call from within the Veil "Ephphatha." I AM open. I am returning to myself—my true self. I am re-discovering all of the facets of my heart. I am most surely attuning to the Sacred within me. I am discerning all of my God-given gifts and who I am. I finally have a better feel for who I am. I like who I'm becoming. I'm finding my way home. I've lived in the center, traveled to the edge, and now I must settle, knowing that the edge and the center are both amazing places to dwell, to travel through, to cross over and back—to simply be. They are precious liminal places in which to become most fully human.

Lyra continued in her soul-searching pseudo-soliloquy. *What or who I am becoming is clearer now, but not yet fully clear to me, and that doesn't matter. That I am becoming is what truly matters. That I am becoming most fully human matters. That my identity is moving from the unclear, towards full clarity matters. That God is with me as I shine brightly matters.*

I know that with all that I've learned today, I believe that my Compassionate Life and my Contemplative Life and my Creative Life stories are slowly merging into one intricately complex and profound storyline. I need time to sift through all of this. My identity is evolving on its own. And, with a little intentional interior work, a little more soul searching of my own, and, a little help from my friends and from my God, my new identity will soon become very clear.

Somehow, I am actually believing that it won't be long at all before it will become wholly, incredibly, crystal clear. God has called out to me to shine. To create in the Light. To use my words. To rise up and shine my creative Light. As Xavad inferred earlier today: In the hush, no need to rush. Like a deer, go forward slowly and surely. Methodically. Masterfully. Meaningfully. No hurry. No worry. Everything in its own time—everything at the right time. In God's time.

Thanks be to God, for all of my learning today, for my seven encounters with the Sacred and the promise of a Sabbath Holy Rest. I am becoming.

She thought about writing down all of her rapid fire and swirling details of the day, but when she picked up her pencil, she just couldn't bring herself to start. She was exhausted. But, she couldn't put her pencil down either. Not yet anyway.

She mused lightheartedly. *After all of my learning and challenges and personal growth and formation today, perhaps I'll become a novelist—become an author. In my newly evolving identity, using all of my God-given gifts, perhaps I'll become known as an author, or a poet, or even as a modern life contemplative! Perhaps I'll write an autobiographical fiction novel, with all of the stories of today as my intriguing chapters and storyline! Hmmmmm . . . .*

Four compelling words—four telling words began dancing and prancing into her consciousness. She felt she'd better quickly write these words down, before they became a nuance of a dream, or a wisp of her imagination, or a breath of nothingness—before they'd be lost forever in her sinking mental exhaustion.

Then she turned the page of her notebook to start a fresh blank page. At the top, in very large boldfaced capital letters, her perfectly poised pencil printed only those four telling words LIGHT BEYOND THE RIVER.

She let out a long-winded sigh, and symbolically put down her pencil. She glanced up at the "Grace is a Way of Life" canvas on the wall, and smiled knowingly. *God works—God responds—in many mysterious ways.* She took a long breath in, and let it out slowly, slowly. A curve of relaxation encircled her frame, leaving her comfortable and calm, warmed and winding down, spiritually suffused and sure.

She reached for the small Connemara stone Celtic Cross standing on the table beside her. She held it in her hand, over her heart. Her other hand rested on Paidi, in her lap. She could feel the warmth of the Holy Lovelight surrounding her now—embracing her weary soul. Her flesh tingled. She tuned in once again to the Holiness of the moment. She sank down deeper into her chair, the back of her head now resting on the chair.

And in that very moment, she knew that something subtle yet something so exquisitely Holy, was happening. Her riverside home, her very own brookside breezeway was becoming a Thin Place—a shimmering translucent interface, perceptibly alive with the Divine Presence of God. It was an indescribable moment, much like her earlier encounter with the veil. Surreal. Sublime. Sacred.

Lyra's fatigue had finally crept into her mind, and her vocabulary was simply failing her.

She held onto the heightened Holiness, and as she lingered in the Light she felt blissfully featherweight. Connected, yet somewhat disconnected. Aloft and floating. Illuminated, yet glowing from within. Awake and attuned, yet nearly asleep. Then, she gently closed her eyes. Her heartbeat slowed. Her breathing slowed and became shallow. There, in her wicker rocking chair on the screened-in-veranda, at her home by the River Saye, aglow in the Holy Lovelight, she fell into a peaceful sleep. The waters of the northside brook babbled quietly as she dreamed. She knew that tomorrow, she could enter into Holy rest with God. She knew she could take time to be Holy, to listen deeply. She was wholly ready to muse into reality, the meaning of those four telling words "LIGHT BEYOND THE RIVER".

The story could simply wind down peacefully, and end right here, with Lyra praying her way into sleep, leaving you to reflect on your own about the directions of Lyra's new pathway and her ever-evolving identity—her becoming most fully human. Or, you can turn the page to enter into, *the Holy Mystery of Light Beyond the River!*

Ephphatha
Paul and Lyra

Throughout my being, my essence, my soul, suffusing all I am,
Reside the mysteries of life, the truth of who I am.
In golden spirals, golden threads, and golden mystic webs,
I rest, I wait, I come to see, the here and now, the next.

Holy Mystery

Lyra had been enjoying the most restorative sleep when the phone rang. She awoke from the depths to the sound of her own cell phone ringing right beside her. She opened one eye and sleepily closed it again. She noted that it was very bright outside. *Morning light*, she inferred in her dazed haze. Lyra was cozy and curled up under a quilt, on her deep-seated rocking chair, on the screened-in veranda. Paidi was in her lap. Choosing to keep her eyes closed, in order to hide away from the sparkling morning brilliance for just a little bit longer, she picked up the phone after the fifth ring and rallied her very best, barely coherent "Good Morning!" to the unknown caller.

"Good Morning, Saint Lyra! This is Paul!"

Instantly springing into wider wakefulness, and with her eyes now voluntarily wide open, Lyra answered "Hey Paul! My Almighty Saint Paul!! It was so good to see you and Crea, out on the trails yesterday. It's been a really long time since we last connected!"

After a brief pause, Paul said slowly, "Lyra, sorry, but we weren't out on any trails. We were both at home looking after our dog after she had had a run in with a fox. Jovi died unfortunately, and we buried her in the woods behind our yard. We're all a little uneasy today, knowing there's a fox lurking near our home."

Lyra listened intently as Paul went on. "We picked some long-stemmed blue asters that were growing there in the woods, and we laid them on her grave. And, just like you would have done Lyra, we stood and said a prayer for her at the graveside."

He paused again. "I'm sure we both, Crea and I, would have really preferred to have been out in the wilds, hiking—especially out to the waterfall. Crea just loves to frolic under the falls. She says she gets all freshilized in there. Sometimes she likes to make up her own words, just for the fun of it. I think she means enlivened! And Crea likes going to the ancient well a lot too. She can while away her time, dangling her feet over the edge of the well. She swears up and down, that after skipping several stones there, she feels radically energized. It's almost like she believes that the waters of the well serve as a natural resource of light, or energy, or some other cosmic spark of vitality, or brain power. She's a smart kid, but sometimes I just shake my head. She has some kid-crazy ideas."

Lyra had been absorbing all that Paul had just said, but her compassionate words came first to her lips. Lyra sat upright, in her rocking chair. She put the call on speakerphone, and she hugged her own sweet Paidi. "Paul, I'm so sorry to hear about your dog. That's awful news. You will miss your wee Jovi for sure! It is so difficult to say a final goodbye to a family pet—especially in such tragic circumstances. Jovi was such a gentle and loving soul. And so young! Ahhhhh, we all love our pets just as much as every other member of our families. You must be so sad." Her voice trailed off. "Blessed be, bonny Jovi, blessed be."

Paul spoke softly, with gratitude. "Thank you for your condolences, Lyra. As ever, you are very, very kind. We do miss our Jovi. She was special."

Lyra paused, acknowledging the gravity of the moment. "But Paul, getting back to yesterday. How can you say you weren't out in the woods with Crea? It was her fourteenth birthday yesterday. She told me herself.

And you took her on a nature walk, back to the Irie Falls! I met you out there totally by chance, and she even lent me her shoes. And Crea is so very right. There is much more to that ancient well than meets the closed and unreceptive heart!"

"Lyra," Paul said, sounding worried. "honest to goodness, we weren't on the woodland trails or at the waterfalls. Or even at the well! Nowhere near there yesterday! And Crea's birthday is in March! Last March! Are you OK? You sound really groggy and confused. Did you fall and hit your head somewhere and knock yourself out?"

Paul continued "I remember Crea talking nonsense a while back, after she struck her head on a rock while chasing the dog in the woods. She got a good concussion back then. She was pretty wide-eyed for a few days. Dazed. And she said something about a shining, or a shimmering over by the pond, whatever that meant. She hasn't mentioned it ever since."

In his deeper, very professional voice, he said "Because of your un-explained confusion this morning Lyra, I should really assess your neuro-logical status, for the accuracy of your orientation in three planes—your current awareness of *person, place and time*. You do know your *name*. That's great. And, you do know your *place*, because you're at home talking to me on the phone. But what about *time*? Do you know what day, and what time of day it is today Lyra?"

"It's Sunday, Paul. Sunday morning for sure. I should be heading off to church in a little while. Look, I have Crea's Crocs here right here beside me, right where I took them off . . . . What? Where? I slipped them off on the mat, right here beside me, before I curled up in my chair, late late late last night. But, they're not here now! Where'd they go?!"

"Lyra, you must have been dreaming. Haha! You say you've misplaced your shoes! Or, as you say, 'Crea's shoes'! Please don't tell me they were glass slippers, and that I should be calling you Cinderella!"

Indignant and imploring, Lyra responded "But Paul, you jokingly called me Cinderella yesterday too! I'm serious! And please, don't start call-ing me Dorothy, and telling me I'm not in Kansas anymore!" There was no tornado yesterday and I didn't hit my head. And yes, I did meet a whole bunch of new BFF's in the forest. They were not the Tin Man, Cowardly Lion and Scarecrow. But they are my newfound best forest friends forever. Zoli, Yala, Bradn, Xavad, and Aorla, Cruith, and Zaba!!! They all taught me some amazing lessons, one by one. And, at the end of the day, we all circle-danced under the stars. And we were all part of a grand moonlit shoreline parade near the midnight hour! It was like a cosmic celebration of wisdom and knowledge. A phantasmagorical festival of enlightenment and spiritual formation. All out there under the grand dome of the universal skies. It was the most extraordinary, and, probably the most memorable day of my whole life! It was a glorified fusion experience of meaning, mystery, and mysticism—of Holy Moments and memories. And best of all, it was the most extreme broadening of my own creative boundaries!"

Reality Check

Paul was clearly worried, because Lyra seemed to be perseverating, in the psychology sense of the word. She was steadfastly clinging—desperately holding on—to her own reality. Paul spoke firmly with his next words. He did a little stern psychological reality-orientation for her.

"Lyra! Wake up! Sit up straight. Feet on the floor. And listen to me. This is a reality check, right here, right now. I think you have awakened from some kind of all-night funky and frivolous dream. Or, perhaps when the phone rang this morning and awakened you from an after-breakfast nap, it jarred you from a very deep REM dream sleep.

"And hear me clearly now. Today—Is—Saturday! 10 a.m.! Check your iPhone for the date! Crea's Crocs are here at our own house, and this is not her birthday weekend! Check your teapot. It's probably full of your favorite cardamom tea. Blazing hot tea at that! I bet you slipped into a wee nap after breakfast, and you've had your crazy dream right there in your comfy chair, after you finished your mug of tea."

Paul was still quite concerned about the source of Lyra's present state of confusion. As a true professional, he was choosing to keep his medical differential diagnosis wide—very very wide. He was still seeking to clarify—to find reason(s) for—her current altered mindset and timeline.

In all seriousness of intent, though in a jovial voice, he said, "Or, maybe, just maybe Lyra, you're just like the little girl in your Sunday School play. Haha! You're living your own dream! If I remember correctly, the title was "She Didn't Say Amen." Young Diarama, prayed to God in the morning, and carried on and on and on in a wonderful and challenging conversation with God. Her morning prayer that day became dream-like. It was about an imaginative journey, a quest, a childhood odyssey of fantasy and faith. And of course in the end, she returned to a newer and changed reality. Diarama's prayer never ended, simply, because she never concluded with saying Amen. By the end, Diarama was unsure of what was, and what wasn't real. She wanted it all to be real.

"Maybe, just maybe, your morning prayer took you away into the depths of a compelling conversation with God. It took you into the farthest reaches of your imagination, into a deep deep deeply contemplative sit, where suspension of reality took over. It took you to a place where you met with, and danced under the stars with, all of your new forest friends.

"Maybe I, should call you 'Diarama'? Maybe *you* didn't close your morning prayer today, with Amen, or simply forgot to say Amen?! Aha! You're slipping, ol' girl! You've got to be careful of what you say, and what you don't say, in your prayers! Someone wise once said 'Be careful what you ask for—it may come your way!'"

He lightened up and laughed playfully "Lyra, my friend, what kind of magic mushrooms did your woodland friends get you into yesterday, back there in the wildwoods?" Paul laughed with gusto. "Maybe yours was actually a psychedelic dream, or a mind-blowing trip?! Maybe I should come by and check your pupils? Haha! Should I check your cardamom stash—maybe its been laced with a powerful hallucinogen??!!? That, would explain your impassioned visions—your moonlit parade of the animals, and your dancing-in-the-river-under-the-stars-at-midnight stories!"

Lyra did not answer Paul. His allusive humor was lost on her. She was checking the calendar on her iPhone. She stared at the tiny screen, and indeed it said Saturday! She felt suddenly stunned. Lost. Crushed. Sent airborne in a dizzy tizzy. Totally out of touch with reality. *Were all of those amazing stories of the day, just a dream? Were all of those Holy Moments, not really real? Were all those moments of Sacred learning and deep contemplation, simply part of an extravagant Odyssean dream, or part of a deep conversation with God? All part of my own poetic projection?! How could I say it was so very tangible and experiential, when the experience didn't even happen?*

She continued to ponder inwardly. *How could all of this have been a dream? Just a dream? The infinitesimally rich details, and the depth of knowledge, and the focus on opening myself and on my becoming, were so real! I'm exasperated! I'm flabbergasted. I can't have just dreamed it! There was so much detail! How could I possibly have taught myself all of the complicated and comprehensive wisdom that I don't already know? I couldn't even begin to contemplate deep enough to make that kind of stuff up. Not unless overnight,*

I've transcended, and I've become some kind of contemplative guru, or a mystic sage, or a scholarly seer!

Truth and Light

And then something occurred to Lyra. She said emphatically into the phone to Paul "I didn't dream it at all!" She was ecstatic. Her heart started to beat a little faster. The words just breathlessly tumbled out of her mouth. "Look! I know, Saint Paul, that you cannot see this over the phone, but I have proof right here that it is real! I can even take an iPhone photo of this, right here, right now, and text it to you, to show you that it is all so real!

"I am telling the truth! Last night, after my walk, here in my chair on the veranda, I wrote down in my notebook, these foretelling—these *four* telling words. They are right here in my notebook! These are the four special words that came swirling around in my mind, at the end of the day. I think these four little words are going to be the beginning of something big. Something very special for me. They will help me to muse my way into clarity, into my future, into my new identity. Who knows what pathways they'll take me along! Saint Paul, my Almighty doctor-friend along the road, please please please hear me out! These words are visionary words. They are life-changing life-blessing Damascus-like eye-opening words, for sure! These four words were given to me just last night. The words are written right here, just like I said."

Lyra put on her reading glasses, and she held up her notebook in front of her face, at eye level. She held it up with her left hand, noticing for the first time, that her beautiful Celtic braided rose gold bangle bracelet was on her wrist. Just seeing it made her smile, knowingly. She stretched her neck sideways, to allow her long locks to tumble forward onto her chest, freely, loosely, unbound. The glint in Paidi's moonstone collar caught her eye. With a clear and steady voice, she read the words from her notebook to Paul over the phone—the four mystically heralding words that were hand-printed plainly at the top of a fresh blank page:

"LIGHT BEYOND THE RIVER"
The End.

Encountering the Sacred
from the Center to the Edge

I'll journey from my center, my home—out to the farthest edge.
That's where I'll witness every realm—and vow to build my nest.
The River, Lovelight, Celtic Thin Place—three muses I hold dear—
I'm called to listen, poised to hear—the music of the spheres.

Ahhhhhh—Home sweet home! We can feel completely centered and balanced, complacent and comfortable in our own homes. There are times though, when we do walk away from our own personal centers, and we find ourselves at our own personal extreme fringe areas, or edges—the edges of our knowing, of our comprehension, of our reality, of our faith, and of our world as we thought we knew it. The edge can be a place of intense stirring, with a smoldering cloud of overwhelm and a somewhat frightening field of vision. Or, it can be an awe-inspiring string of moments full of wonderment and surprise. Or even still, it can be a calming and self-completing call—calling us onward into the unknown. We can rise up and answer the call to the edge when we first hear it, or we can choose to venture there when and if an inner sense of readiness arises in our peregrinating spirit.

We can choose to resettle ourselves out there, precariously at the edge, and then live in the hope that while we're still out there we'll once again regain that centered feeling, that balance, equilibrium, homeostasis, and that deep inner peace and contentment we once knew at home. Or, we can choose to return to our original center, our old home, equipped with our new knowledge and experiential lessons, and new visions and muses—we can return to our homes, forever changed. We can coddiwomple and find our way, or we can envision and make a plan.

To journey from the center to the edge, and back again, is most certainly a life-changing and a life-giving experience. Choosing to live at the center, or at the edge, is simply a personal choice only to be made for ourselves, by ourselves, in our own time, at the right time—and only if and when we are fully open to our whole selves—only if and when we are intentionally open to our own wide worlds.

We can extrapolate the words of the ancient Ecclesiastes Scripture ....

There is a time for every purpose under heaven.
A time at the center—A time at the edge
A time to muse—A time to voice
A time to be—A time to become
A time to shine—A time to shine brightly.

We are human. And we are uniquely and beautifully woven and knit and laced and stitched with all colors and textures and tensions of cords and threads and yarns. Some of our threads are scholarly, theological, contemplative, spiritual, mystical, in plain sight and matter of fact, or even shadowy and mysterious, creative, compassionate, iridescent—shining bright. Everyone's weave, or knit—or crochet or tat—is most surely one of a kind.

As humans, we are inherently graced by the Sacred—by That/Which/ Whom dwells deep within our being. We are born in original blessing, and born of essential goodness. We live in a world that is *of God*, and we indeed are *of God*. We are Light. We are Holy. We are Sacred.

As humans, we have the capacity to learn, to grow, and to become. What or who or how we become is only a part of the journey from the center, to the edge, and perhaps back again. In all of our journeys we can venture into our interior world where we can all find our center. We can all find our way home, with God as our True North, our Waypoint, our traveling companion, our friend on the journey. We can encounter the Sacred in many ways, in many places, in many realms, along the way. We can all arrive safely, at our own home sweet home.

Thanks be to God. Amen.

My Closing Prayer

O God of my heart—
O God of the Light of the earth and sky—
O God of the River of cresting grace—
Please hear my humble prayer.
Help me to look to the Light Beyond the River,
and to answer its fervent call.
Let me river on with You, in this Light,
with openness of eyes, mind, heart, faith and trust—
opening and expanding all of my personal limits
and my creative boundaries—
that I might choose to rise up and respond
to the ever-present Sacredness in all of Creation—
that I might be transformed—that I may transcend—
that I may become most fully human—
as I attune to the Holy, both in my midst, and, deep within.
May I know no limits in myself, in my world, or in You, my God.
And, in the newly evolving identity of me,
may I ever humbly serve You, with a Servant Heart.
The Holy Lovelight graces me,
and my grateful heart
sings and shines—
shines brightly !!!
O God of Holy Ever-presence—
O God of the running waves upon the shore—
I offer my gratitude—
I offer myself to You.
Amen.

Acknowledgments

With heartfelt gratitude

To my sister, Brenda
for her inborn and sensitive insights into humanity

To all of my parents and grandparents
for teaching me, believing in me—for leading me onward through their wisdom

To my doctor-friend, Paul
for his faith—and his trust—in me
for his deep and abiding faith and trust—in God

To my friend, John
who daily, embodied the Living Faith, long before I even understood the term

To my cousin, Rodney
for his open, seeking spirit

To my church friend—friend of the faith, Peter
who through his integrity, diplomacy, and his living example,
taught me, that in reserve of word, generative silence can speak,
and, that deep listening can truly befriend

To my pilgrim friend, Julie
for the opportunity to live vicariously through her, by the waters at the Well of Dun I,
where her depths met with—and became one with—mine

To George
for sharing his vulnerability,
for showing his gratitude—plainly, freely, intentionally

To my mentor, Kirk Wipper, CM
who truly opened my eyes

To The Reverend Wanda Stride MDiv
who lives and breathes—and who simply is—
faith, music, and passion for all of life and living

To The Reverend Patricia Gale-MacDonald MDiv
whose wide-open faith and personal witness of social justice and loving
kindness, led me in my Compassionate Life, to walk so very closely with
my God

To The Reverend Dr Colin MacDonald PhD
whose own deep love for Christ literally launched me on an ever-evolving
Pauline-style Spiritual Formation Journey, and a lifelong odyssey in
Christlike Living
and, who honored—and made space for—my poetic and contemplative
queries into the realm of the Holy Lovelight

To Dr John Philip Newell PhD, Author
whose writings and wisdom nurtured my formative journey as a Celtic
Christian,
and who over time, taught my heart to see

To Spiritual Director, Jan Evans MA Spiritual Formation
whose own Holy Listening empowered me in my discernment journey
to articulate my story—to articulate my faith—to articulate my own
becoming

To Spiritual Director, Wendy Passmore MA Ministry and Spirituality
who listened, and heard me—who attunes to and celebrates, all good gifts

To Stephen Sims, Author
who affirmed my journey, my place on the river

To Dr David G. Benner PhD, Author
whose words and works un-scattered my own thoughts and visions,
enabling me to speak out my own story of "becoming most fully human"

To all of my friends on the journey, and my friends of the faith
who believed in me, and who validated my contemplative soul—
who encouraged me to continue writing from the heart—
who taught me to open myself, and, to listen—
these folks, are my village—they raised me up up up

For all of the subtle and not-so-subtle spiritual and mystical nudges
that bombarded me in 2019–2022,
in my own personal Pentecost—in my own personal Peniel—
to open my creative boundaries wide enough
for me to consider writing for the first time in fiction form

To Sallie Vandagrift, Editor
for her thoughtful and diligent attention to detail
for her wordsmithing powers,
and her mentoring spirit in "working with" my vision, with grace

And last, but truly first, to my husband Barry
who so freely gives me all of the space I need, to live in my creative, contemplative world
With him, I am intimately known, loved, and understood
In his love, I am whole

My hugs, and heartfelt "Thank You!" to all of you. God bless you.
May the peace of the gentle running waves on the shore,
ever lull you—ever call you—into the breath of Amen.
Amen.

About the Author

For more information about Janis Constable and her other books,
visit her website—her new and evolving author website
www.janisconstablebooks.com

P.S.

Fictional character "Lyra" went on—in real life as Janis Constable—
to become a published author.
She wrote the fiction novel, *Light Beyond The River* and two contemplative
prose collections,
Random and Nebulous and *My Indulgent Interior Life*.
One day—someday—just maybe someday—her dream will come true
and she'll finally compile her treasured music compositions
in a themed hymnbook trilogy,
Lovelight and the Living Faith.
All of her works are intricately interlaced
with her Celtic Christian Wisdom, her love of God,
and her delightful contemplative prosetry.
Janis' life is full of Light.
Janis is Light.
Janis today is truly, shining brightly.